★ GREAT IRISH SPORTS STARS

JASON
SHERLOCK

DONNY MAHONEY is a writer and journalist. He was born in America and has lived in Ireland since 2004. He is one of the co-founders of the website Balls.ie, where he works today. He is the author of *Great Irish Sports Stars: Colm 'Gooch' Cooper* and *Aim High: Irish Sports Stars, Trailblazers and Mavericks*, illustrated by Eoin Coveney.

GREAT IRISH SPORTS STARS

JASON SHERLOCK

DONNY MAHONEY

THE O'BRIEN PRESS
DUBLIN

First published 2021 by
The O'Brien Press Ltd,
12 Terenure Road East, Rathgar,
Dublin 6, Ireland
D06 HD27
Tel: +353 1 4923333; Fax: +353 1 4922777
E-mail: books@obrien.ie
Website: www.obrien.ie
The O'Brien Press is a member of Publishing Ireland.

ISBN: 978-1-78849-252-2

8 7 6 5 4 3 2 1
23 22 21

Printed and bound in Great Britain by Clays Ltd, Elcograf S.p.A.
The paper in this book is produced using pulp from managed forests.

Published in:

DUBLIN
UNESCO
City of Literature

CONTENTS

CHAPTER I

WELCOME TO FINGLAS

It was a Saturday afternoon in 1983. A seven-year-old boy named Jason Sherlock stood outside the front door of his house in Finglas in Dublin. He looked around his estate. Birds were singing. The sun was shining. Boys and girls were outside playing football.

Life is just brilliant, he thought.

'Mam, hurry! I don't want to be late for the match!' Jason shouted back into the house.

They had plenty of time, but Jason didn't want to be a second late.

'One second,' his mam Alice shouted back.

Jason had black hair, which he combed forward. He was wearing a sky-blue football kit. If you were new to the area, you might have thought Jason was wearing the kit of the Dublin Gaelic football team. In fact, Jason was wearing the kit of Rivermount Boys FC, his local football club.

Jason and the Rivermount Boys had a huge match this afternoon against one of the other big schoolboy clubs in Finglas. His mam was going to walk him to the pitch.

'All ready,' his mam said, as she put her coat on. 'Shall we?'

Jason's mam extended her hand out and Jason reached out and grabbed it. Together they walked through their estate to the nearby football pitch at Tolka Valley Park. Jason loved his mam. He felt so lucky to have the best mam in the world.

They lived in a semi-detached house in an estate called Carrigallen Park. Jason lived with his mam Alice, his nan, Kathleen, his Uncle Eddie and his Uncle Brian. Jason didn't have any siblings, but he didn't mind, because Carrigallen Park was full of kids his age. One side of his house were the Geraghtys: they had five kids. On the other side were the Cahills. They had five kids as well. He was never stuck for someone to play football with in

Carrigallen Park.

'Will you score me a goal today, Jason?' she said.

'Absolutely,' he replied.

As Jason and his mam walked to the football pitch, Jason's best mate from the estate, Pato, sprinted over from the green with a football in his hand.

'Jason! Jason!' he shouted. 'Would you have time for a quick game of Wembley?' Pato said.

'No, sorry, Pato, we have a big match at 3pm today,' Jason said.

'No worries,' Pato said.

'After the match, though, Pato,' Jason's mam said.

'Sure thing, Mrs Sherlock. Good luck in the match, Jay,' Pato said.

'Thanks!' Jason shouted.

Sport was Jason's favourite thing in the whole world. Through sport, Jason made amazing friends. He would play *literally* anything. He'd recently tried tennis out and absolutely loved it. Give him a golf club and he'd be hitting wedges like he was playing in the Irish Open.

He played up front for the Rivermount Boys. Their youngest team was under-11s so Jason's teammates were all bigger and older than him. He didn't mind.

He and his mam arrived at the pitch. The River-mount lads were at one end, taking shots on goal.

'Wish me luck, Mam.'

'You can do it, Jason.'

His mam believed in him, and that gave him so much confidence. He wanted to make her so proud of him. He sprinted at full speed to join the lads.

'Great to see you, Jason,' said his coach Joe. 'Loosen up a bit before we kick off. We've got a big game today!'

'Sure thing, Joe!' Jason said. Joe was a really inspiring coach. Jason didn't want to let him down.

Even though Jason was the smallest kid on the pitch, he was still one of Rivermount's most dangerous players. He was lightning quick.

In the second half, Jason even scored that goal for his mam.

All of his teammates surrounded him after the goal to congratulate him.

'Good man Jason!' Coach Joe shouted from the sidelines. Jason could see his mam clapping excitedly on the sideline. She looked delighted. He gave her a thumbs up. The match finished a draw.

'You played brilliantly, Jason, well done,' his mam said afterwards.

'Thanks Mam,' he said.

Jason was quiet on the walk back home to Carrigallen Park. While he was delighted to score, he was thinking about something. After the match, Jason noticed the fathers of many of his teammates on the sidelines congratulating their children. Jason's mam, meanwhile, was there on her own. Jason's mam and dad weren't in a relationship, and he rarely saw his dad. This just got Jason thinking.

'Something on your mind, Jason?' she said.

'Mam, I have a question for you,' Jason said. 'Am I different from the other lads?'

'What do you mean? Of course not. Wherever did you get that idea?'

It had been on his mind recently. Unlike a lot of the kids he knew, Jason didn't have any brothers or sisters. He didn't mind that so much because his family loved him so much. Also, Jason's dad was Chinese and from Hong Kong, so Jason looked a little bit different to the other kids in the estate.

'I was just wondering,' Jason said. 'Our family seems different to some of the others in the estate.'

'Ah no, Jason. We're all the same. We're all human beings, no one is different, no matter where you come from or how you look.'

'Thanks mam,' Jason said. This made him feel much better.

'You're just an ordinary boy from Finglas,' she said. 'Actually no, you're not just an ordinary boy. You're an *extraordinary* boy from Finglas!'

Jason was delighted now. His mam made him feel like he could achieve anything.

CHAPTER 2

ON THE HANDLEBARS WITH
UNCLE BRIAN

It was a beautiful Saturday afternoon in September. Jason was outside his house in Finglas, soloing a football. He was seven now.

'Ten, eleven, twelve and thirteen…' Jason said. He was practising every day and getting better at keeping the ball off the ground.

Uncle Brian came out of the house. He was wearing the kit of Kinvara Boys, one of the big local football clubs. He held a plastic bag from Dunnes with a pair of football boots inside.

'It's a grand day to play football!' he said. 'Will we head soon?'

'Ready when you are,' Jason said. He loved going to his uncle's football games.

'Lovely, I'll grab the *rothar.*'

Uncle Brian and Uncle Eddie were both in their thirties. Neither of them were married or had any kids. Which meant they had loads of time for Jason. They'd join in for kickarounds with Jason and watch *Match of Day* and *The Sunday Game* with him. His uncles were big Dublin GAA supporters and they'd taken Jason all around the country to support the Dublin Gaelic football team.

As Jason was waiting, his nan walked out the front door.

'Come here to me before you go, Jason,' his nan said. 'I have something for you.'

She had a twinkle in her eye. Jason's nan had been to the shops that afternoon. She often brought him home a treat.

'Here's a little something for you for being the best grandson,' she said, reaching deep into her handbag. She pulled a packet of Maltesers out.

'Thanks, Nanny!' he said. He opened the packet, tasted one and then put the rest in his jacket pocket for later.

'Now give me a hug,' she said. Jason didn't hesitate. She was a great nan, one of the world's best nans.

Jason's nan was born in Laois and moved to Dublin when she was young. Jason's mam and her brothers grew up not far away from Carrigallen Park, in a place called Phibsboro. They'd all moved to Carrigallen Park together before Jason was born.

Uncle Brian emerged from the back of the house with his racing bike.

'Let's go so, Jay. Kickoff is in a half hour.'

Jason climbed on top of the handlebars. Uncle Brian cycled to all of his matches. Jason was his biggest fan and he travelled with him to all of his matches atop the handlebars of his bike.

Just as they were about to leave, Jason's mam came out the front door.

'Jason, you'll behave yourself during the match, won't you? Don't go running off anywhere,' she said.

'Don't worry, Mam,' she said. 'I just want to watch a game of football.'

'All right so,' she said and waved them off. Jason's mam was always a little bit worried about him. He loved that about her.

Today Kinvara Boys had a match at Albert College Park in Ballymun. It was a fifteen minute bike ride from Carrigallen Park. Riding with Uncle Brian was one of the greatest feelings in the world. It was such a brilliant buzz to have the wind blowing in his face as his uncle raced the bike along. They'd fly past people waiting for the bus or minding the front garden. It made Jason feel like a superhero.

'All right Jason, ready for the quiz?' Uncle Brian said.

'Yes!' Jason said. Uncle Brian would always ask Jason questions about football when they cycled.

'What's a nutmeg?' he said.

'When you kick the ball through a player's legs,' Jason said.

'A1,' Uncle Brian said. 'What's a bicycle kick?'

'When you jump up and meet a cross with an overhead kick and land on your back.'

'Good man. Now what's a rabona?'

'A rabona is when you take your kicking foot and put it behind your bad leg to kick the ball.'

'You aced the test!' Uncle Brian said.

Jason was delighted. He was becoming a football

expert. He really loved the outrageous bits of skill that some players could do.

Cycling down the road, chatting about football to his uncle, Jason was in seventh heaven. He couldn't think of anything better in the whole world than watching a game of football on a Saturday afternoon in Dublin. He'd gained his passion for sport from his uncles. They loved football, they loved Dublin GAA, they loved all sport, really.

As they reached the park, they cycled past a sign that read 'Na Fianna GAA club wishes Dublin the best of luck in the 1983 All-Ireland'. Dublin were playing Galway in the All-Ireland final in two weeks time. It was Jason's secret hope that his uncles would get him tickets for the game so they could all support Dublin. But Jason knew it was impossible.

'Still on the look out for those tickets for the All-Ireland,' Uncle Brian said. 'They're like gold dust.'

'I understand,' Jason said, trying not to sound disappointed.

'I'll score a goal for you, Jason,' Uncle Brian said, when they arrived at the pitch.

'Good luck!' Jason shouted. Uncle Brian played as a centre back so Jason knew this was extremely unlikely.

Jason found a spot on the sideline and sat down to watch the game. He reached into his pocket, and remembered the packet of Maltesers that his nan gave him. She really was the best nan in the world!

The match was entertaining. It might not have been Manchester United versus Liverpool at Old Trafford in terms of quality, but the players took it just as seriously. There were old lads and young lads playing in the match and the thing they had in common was their love of football. Jason could see how happy the men were when playing the game. Although, when they were angry, they weren't shy about letting their teammates or the referee know about it!

The whole park was full of people playing different sports. Sport seemed to make the whole world go around. Jason loved that.

The match finished nil-all and the two teams shook hands at the full-time whistle.

'I owe you a goal,' Uncle Brian said, slightly disappointed.

'Maybe next week!' Jason said.

'I'll get you a choc ice to make up for it,' Uncle

Brian said.

'Thanks!' Jason said. A choc ice and a pack of Maltesers in the same afternoon: it was working out to be a good day!

CHAPTER 3

THE 1983 ALL-IRELAND FINAL

Carrigallen Park was full of anticipation. The blue and navy bunting was out. Dublin flags hung from lampposts and car antennas. The Boys in Blue would play in the All-Ireland football final in just two days. That Sunday, Dublin would take on Galway for the right to lift Sam Maguire.

Just before dinner, Uncle Eddie rushed into the house full of excitement.

'Guess what, Jason?' he said, 'I've got some great news.'

'What is it?' Jason asked.

'I've got tickets for the All-Ireland on Sunday.'

Uncle Eddie and Jason jumped up and down like they'd scored a goal for Dublin.

'There's one catch,' Eddie said. 'They're Hill 16 tickets. It's going to be cramped, and you might not have a great view of the match, but it'll be an amazing day.'

Hill 16 was where all of the serious Dublin supporters went during Dublin games. Jason considered himself a serious Dublin supporter. But there were no seats, and Jason was just a small lad.

'I don't care,' Jason said. 'I just want to be at Croke Park on Sunday.'

'But how will Jason see the game?' Jason's mam said. 'There's no seats in Hill 16. Everyone has to stand to see the game.'

Jason's mam had a good point.

'Don't worry. I have a solution,' Uncle Eddie said. 'Shouldervision! You can go on my shoulders, it'll be grand,' he said, lifting Jason up over his head.

'Brilliant,' Jason said.

'How far can you see?' Uncle Eddie said.

'An awful long way!' Jason said.

Jason's mam didn't seem convinced.

'Will you be able to hold him up there for two hours?' she said.

'A strapping young man like me, of course!'

he said.

She didn't seem certain, but she could see how badly Jason wanted to go.

'You might need a pair of binoculars as well!' she said.

Jason was so happy. There was a special feeling about this All-Ireland because Kerry weren't involved. Kerry had played in the last five All-Irelands and people were happy to see some different teams in the final. It had been six years since Dublin had won an All-Ireland and GAA fans in the capital were desperate to keep Sam Maguire at home.

Jason loved the Dublin football team. They were managed by the great Kevin Heffernan. The Dublin fans all called him 'Heffo'. The Dublin supporters called themselves Heffo's Army.

Jason and his uncles had been part of Heffo's Army a few times that season. Eddie had brought Jason to the All-Ireland semifinal against Cork. That day they had amazing seats in the Hogan Stand, just a few rows back from the sideline. It was an incredible place to see a match from. Jason could hear all the noise echoing around the stadium. He could see Heffo studying the match from the sideline and all the intricate movements from the players and off-the-ball incidents that you'd never see on TV. It was about as close to the game you could get without being selected to play in it.

The match had finished a draw and Dublin had to travel to Cork for the replay. Thankfully, they'd won that and now they were just seventy minutes from glory.

Jason idolised all the players in the Dublin team: the likes of Barney Rock and Kieran Duff and Brian Mullins. They were Jason's heroes. They'd grown up not far from him and were wearing the blue jersey in Croke Park. Even though Jason didn't play much Gaelic football, he loved the Dublin kit. He loved the bright blue Dublin jersey and the navy blue shorts. He loved the crest on the shirt, with the three castles burning.

On All-Ireland final day, Jason and Uncle Eddie had a big feed before setting off for Croke Park. Thankfully, the stadium was only a few kilometres from their house. As they got closer to Croke Park, the streets filled with people. Along the Royal Canal, and on the Clonliffe Road, it was thronged with GAA supporters.

Ladies with Dublin accents called out, 'Hats, scarves, headbands! Get your hats, scarves and headbands!'

It was so noisy. The guards were there, directing pedestrian traffic.

'Hold my hand, son,' Uncle Eddie said.

Jason held on tight. He didn't want to lose his uncle and miss the match!

This was unlike any other sporting event he'd ever been to. There was a feeling of electricity in the air. Sam Maguire was at stake. There were loads of fans from Galway there, wearing maroon and white. They wanted their county to win as badly as the Dublin fans wanted the Boys in Blue to win. Jason couldn't even imagine what it would be like if Dublin lost today. He'd be sick!

Finally, Jason and Uncle Eddie reached the Hill 16 Entrance to Croke Park on Jones's Road.

Uncle Eddie reached into his pocket.

'Here you go, Jason. The golden ticket!'

Jason took a look at the ticket. It read '1983 All-Ireland football final: Dublin v Galway. Hill 16 Entrance'.

They joined the queue for Hill 16, or the Hill, as all the Dublin fans referred to it. The Hill was a sacred place for Dublin GAA supporters. It was a standing-only terrace similar to what you'd find in soccer stadiums. And the Dublin supporters sang like they were at a soccer game. Their favourite songs were 'Molly Malone' and 'Dublin in the Rare Auld Times'.

A lot of GAA fans from down the country hated the Hill, but the Dublin supporters made it their home.

Eventually they reached the entrance of the stadium. A steward checked Jason's ticket and let him in. It was such an amazing feeling to be inside the stadium. All of Ireland would be watching the match. Irish people all around the world would be watching or listening to the radio commentary. Only 70,000 people, including the Taoiseach, were lucky enough to get a ticket into the stadium. Jason was one of those lucky people.

Uncle Eddie found a place in the stand. They were packed in like sardines. Jason couldn't see far past the other much-taller supporters.

'Jump up on my shoulders, Jason,' Uncle Eddie

said.

His uncle lifted him up and put him right on his shoulders. Jason could see all of the beautiful Croke Park pitch now! Uncle Eddie wasn't the tallest man in the world, but Jason could see everything he needed.

'Thanks Uncle Eddie! This is brilliant. I can see everything.'

'Lovely,' Uncle Eddie said. 'I'll need you to keep me updated on what happens on the pitch because I can't see so well myself!'

'No problem!' Jason said.

Jason felt goosebumps as the two teams paraded around Croke Park, led by the Artane Band. All the fans in the stadium rose to salute the teams and a huge noise – a noise louder than anything he had ever heard in his whole life – filled Croke Park.

Jason felt so lucky to be there. He was bursting with pride to be from Dublin and supporting the Boys in Blue.

It was clear not long after throw-in that it was going to be a tough, scrappy match. There was pushing and shoving from both teams. Jason kept Uncle Eddie up-to-date with every important kick of the ball.

About twenty minutes into the game Dublin scored a goal out of the blue!

'What happened, what happened, what happened?' Uncle Eddie said.

'It's one of the maddest goals you'll ever see. It was a Galway kickout. The Galway keeper kicked it right to Kieran Duff. Duffer shot from about 30 yards and scored!'

There was more punching and kicking between the teams. During half-time, the stadium announcer announced that a few players had been sent off because of a scrap in the tunnel. Dublin had a small point lead, but were hanging on for dear life.

A tall man, who was standing right beside them, tapped Uncle Eddie on the shoulder, during half-time.

'I'll take the young fella for the second half,' he said.

'Are you sure?' Uncle Eddie said.

'Absolutely, no bother.'

With that, Jason jumped on the shoulders of this total stranger. Uncle Eddie looked relieved. His back was starting to give way.

In the second half, there were more red cards. Dublin went down to twelve men!

The teams scrapped and scrapped and when the referee blew the final whistle, the Hill exploded with joy. Dublin had held their lead and were All-Ireland champions, winning 1-10 to 1-08.

Dublin fans started singing 'Molly Malone' and Jason joined in.

'Crying cockles and mussels, alive, alive ohhhhh…'

A few days after, the Dublin supporters held a big reception at a fancy hotel in the Dublin city centre and Jason was determined to go. Uncle Brian and Uncle Eddie were going because they went to all of the Dublin games. The Sam Maguire was going to be there, and possibly some Dublin players as well.

'You have to let me go, Mam,' Jason said. 'These are my heroes.'

'Do you promise to behave for Uncle Brian and Uncle Eddie?'

'Of course, I do!'

'Okay you can go, but it's a fancy event, so you'll have to dress up,' his mam said.

Dublin winning the All-Ireland was the biggest thing that had happened in his life. Jason didn't want to attend the ceremony dressed in any old thing. So he took his communion suit out of his wardrobe and put on the white pants and white shirt.

'I'm ready,' Jason said, showing his outfit to his family.

'You're the real deal, Jason!' his mam said.

'Very sharp,' Jason's nan said.

They looked so proud of him when he was dressed up in a suit and tie.

There was a great atmosphere at the reception. The Dubs had kept Sam Maguire in the capital and all the supporters were delighted. The Sam Maguire trophy was presented to the fans and supporters were allowed to take photos with it. It was the biggest trophy Jason had ever seen. It was silver and shiny. Jason could sit in it if he wanted to. He tried to lift it, but he couldn't! It was *that* heavy.

'You know who's here?' Uncle Eddie said.

'Tell me,' Jason said.

'Kevin Moran!'

'Wow!' Jason said. Kevin Moran played football with Manchester United. But he'd also played with Dublin on the team that won the All-Ireland in 1976 and 1977. He was the only sportsman who'd lifted the FA Cup and the Sam Maguire trophy.

'Will we get a photograph with him?' Eddie said.

'Definitely,' Jason said.

They approached him at his table.

'Kevin, howaya, I just wanted to introduce my nephew Jason to you. He's a talented soccer player and a huge Dublin fan. I was wondering if we could get a photograph with you.'

'Absolutely,' Kevin said. Kevin was a big, tall centre back, but a really nice guy.

They posed for the photo.

'So you're a footballer?' Kevin said to Jason. 'Will you be joining me at Manchester United some day?'

'Maybe if you join Liverpool!' Jason said with a laugh.

Kevin pretended to be insulted, and then shook Eddie's hand after the photo was taken. It was amazing to meet a real-life Manchester United player from Dublin. If Kevin Moran could make it in England, Jason thought he could too.

Some day that will be me, Jason thought.

CHAPTER 4

MEAN STREETS

It was a warm, sunny summer's day. Jason was eight-years-old. Jason and his friend Pato from Carrigallen Park were looking to find a few lads for a game of football, but no one in the estate was around.

'They're all gone down the country,' Jason said.

'Let's go find a game,' Pato said.

Jason liked the sound of that.

They wandered and wandered through the estates of Finglas. Finally after about a half hour of walking, they found a few lads playing a game of World Cup. Jason didn't know any of them to see. They were a bit older and bigger than he was. Jason didn't mind, he liked the challenge of taking on the bigger kids.

'Can we join in?' Jason asked.

'Sure,' said one of the lads. 'We have even numbers, so you'll have to play on different teams.'

'Fine by us,' Jason said. He marked Pato for a while, and vice versa.

It was a rough game, with loads of slide tackles, but that made it fun. There was a lad wearing the Netherlands national jersey on the opposite team to Jason who looked a bit scary.

'Watch Netherlands,' Pato whispered to Jason. 'He's a bit of a head the ball.'

Jason nodded. A few minutes later, Jason got the ball with just Netherlands to beat to score a goal. Netherlands sprinted at him. He dove and tried to take his ankles out. Jason could feel the fear rising, but before he could even think twice, he dinked the ball over the sliding defender and stepped around his challenger.

He was free on goal now and he easily slotted past the keeper.

All the other kids screamed and shouted. It was a brilliantly taken goal, but all the lads started giving the lad in the Netherlands shirt abuse for missing the tackle.

'The short lad made you look like an absolute fool,' one of the kids said.

The lad with the Netherlands shirt pulled himself off the ground. His face was red. He was raging.

Jason was feeling great for scoring the goal, but he quickly felt very nervous. There might be repercussions.

The next time the ball came Jason's way, the Netherlands lad made no mistake about it. He tackled Jason hard, not even getting the ball. It would have been a red-card offense if there were referees around.

Jason lay on the pitch, grabbing his shin. He was in serious pain.

'How does that feel?' the kid shouted at Jason, as Jason looked up from the ground. 'Go back to your own country.'

For a split second, Jason froze. He couldn't believe what had been said to him. The words cut him like a knife. He felt so angry and the only thing he knew what to do was jump off the ground and fight the lad with the Netherlands shirt. He was twice the size of Jason. Jason threw a few punches and tried to wrestle him to the ground. Netherlands fought back. Eventually Pato pulled Jason from the scrap.

'Come on, come on,' Pato said. 'Let's just leave these clowns alone.'

Jason dusted himself off. He had a few scratches from the fight. His anger had quietened, but he still felt adrenaline from being in the scrap. The lads shouted something as they walked away but Jason and Pato couldn't really hear it. Jason just wanted to get home

It was a really long walk back to their estate. The whole way back, Jason remained quiet. He didn't want to talk. He felt really embarrassed, but he couldn't explain why. Anytime Jason remembered what the kid in the Netherlands shirt had said, and the hatred in his voice, the anger flashed up inside him again. But Jason also felt guilty, like he had done something wrong. Jason thought about the incident over and over, and tried to figure out what he had done wrong, but nothing came to mind.

Finally they arrived back at Carrigallen Park.

'Let's never go back there to play football,' Jason said.

'No chance,' Pato said.

Jason felt so lucky to have a mate like Pato, who he knew he could rely on in any situation.

'Did you have a good day?' Nanny said.

'It was okay,' Jason said, and ran up to his room. He read football magazines, but felt sad. He stayed up in his room until his mam called him to come down for dinner.

'You're very quiet tonight,' his mam said. 'You're barely touching your food. Did something happen today?'

'No,' Jason said.

'Where did you go with Pato?' she asked.

'I don't want to talk about it,' Jason said; he played with his food until his mam let him go back to his room.

As Jason tried to sleep that night, he remembered the incident with the kid in the Netherlands shirt again. He wasn't going to let someone hurt him in the same way ever again.

A few days later, Jason's mam asked him to go and get some shopping.

'Here's ten quid,' Jason's mam said. 'Will you get us a litre of milk and a bag of spuds? And you can get yourself a choc ice while you're down there.'

'Sure,' Jason said.

The shop was just up the road.

A few kids he recognised from the other side of the estate were outside the shop milling about, eating crisps. Jason didn't really know them. They were bigger than he was, and looked a bit scary.

'Hey, look who just arrived from China,' a lad named Mike said as Jason walked by them. All the lads around him burst out laughing.

Jason wouldn't stand for it. He jumped onto Mike and wrestled him to the ground. There were some punches thrown before the lads pulled him apart. Jason's shirt got stretched at the neck. There was no way he was going to be able to hide this from his mam.

'What happened to you?' she said as soon as she saw him. She was shocked.

'I got in a scrap with a lad outside the shop,' Jason said.

'Over what?' Jason's mam asked.

Jason wouldn't answer. Jason didn't know what to say. He didn't know how to talk about what had happened outside the shop. Mike had wanted to make him feel like he was different, and that he didn't belong.

'Who was it then?' she said.

'Mike from the other side of the estate.

'Well I'm going to go sort this out with Mike's mam.'

She stormed out of the house.

She came back fifteen minutes later. She didn't seem happy.

'Jason, I don't know what these rows are about but I don't like it.'

Jason didn't like it either. But he didn't want to talk about it. Not with his mam, not with anyone. He kept it all to himself.

CHAPTER 5

A VISIT TO A CHINESE RESTAURANT IN DUBLIN

It was the day of the Merseyside derby: Jason's beloved Liverpool were playing Everton. Jason was only eight, but he still understood the significance of the fixture.

Jason was not in good humour. He and Mam were travelling into Dublin city centre on the bus. Jason usually loved travelling into town, but not today. He and his mam were going to visit Jason's dad's family to have dinner together.

The family were Chinese. They'd come to Ireland from Hong Kong and ran a Chinese restaurant, just off Grafton Street, in the heart of the city centre.

Ireland was a different country then. In 1984, generally speaking, the only people who lived in Ireland had been born in Ireland. All of Jason's friends had family who lived in London or Boston or Sydney. But the idea of someone from far away coming to live in Ireland was unheard of. Jason's dad's family were the exception.

'Are you looking forward to meeting your dad's family?' Jason's mam asked as they waited for the bus.

Jason shrugged his shoulders.

'I wish I could stay home and watch Liverpool.'

'I know you love Liverpool, but it's important to spend time with family. We can watch the highlights tonight.'

Jason's mam and dad weren't in a relationship. Jason's dad had moved abroad for work and Jason didn't see him that much. Every now and again, Jason would spend time with his dad's family in Dublin. They'd always have a nice time.

The double-decker bus arrived. Jason and his mam climbed the tall stairs of the bus and took a seat on the top deck. As Jason walked down the aisle, he was aware that he looked a little bit different from everyone else. He could feel a few people looking at him. It wasn't a nice feeling: to be made to feel different.

One thing was for sure: he didn't feel any different. He knew he was the same as all the other kids in Finglas. He loved sport like they did. His accent was exactly the same as theirs. He loved the Dublin Gaelic football team like they did. Jason was a Dub. True blue.

It took twenty minutes to get into the city centre. Jason's mam held his hand on the bus, and it made him feel safe.

'Here's our stop,' his mam said when they reached College Green. 'Hope you're hungry, they're going to have a lovely meal for us.'

They always met at the family restaurant. It was one way that Jason could get familiar with the traditions of his dad's family.

But when he met his dad's family, he was reminded that he had another side to him.

Jason's uncle was named Martin. He was waiting for them outside the restaurant.

'Hi, Jason,' Martin said, and hugged him.

'Hi,' Jason said bashfully.

'Will we get some food?' Martin asked.

'Sure,' Jason's mam said.

The whole family was there to greet them at the entrance. Martin's mam – Jason's nan – came over and gave Jason a big hug. Her English wasn't so great, but she was full of affection for Jason. She handed them menus as well.

'What would you like to eat, Jason?' Martin said.

Jason looked at the menu. There were a lot of Chinese dishes he didn't know. He didn't like the look of most of them.

'This is some of the best Chinese food in the country,' his mam said. 'What will you have, Jason?'

Jason didn't want to eat any Chinese food.

'I want fish and chips,' Jason said.

'Are you sure?' his mam said. She looked disappointed. 'Chinese food is really delicious.'

'Yes, I'm one hundred percent sure. I'll have fish and chips,' Jason said.

It was simple in Jason's mind. If he ate Irish food, he was Irish. If he ate Chinese food, it meant he was Chinese.

'Okay, so,' Jason's mam said.

'No problem,' Martin said. 'We make a really nice

fish and chips as well.'

Jason's mam and Martin chatted away. When the food came, Martin ate all of his food with chopsticks. His mam ate her food with a knife and fork.

'I could teach you how to eat with chopsticks if you want, Jason,' his uncle said.

'No thanks,' Jason said.

His mam looked disappointed in him, but Jason didn't care. He knew what he liked and what he didn't like. The fish and chips were really good.

There was an awkward silence for a minute before Martin spoke up.

'Jason, do you see that TV over there?' he said, pointing to the TV in the corner of the room that was turned off.

'Yeah?' Jason said.

'Well how about I turn on the Liverpool versus Everton match and you can watch it?'

'Really?!' Jason said.

'Really!' Martin said.

He turned the match on. It was the second half, live from Anfield. Jason couldn't have been happier. He might not have seen his dad's family very much, but he knew he was loved.

It was actually pretty nice to have this other side to his family.

CHAPTER 6

THE BEAUTY OF BASKETBALL

I t was a year of change for Jason. He was ten now and in his first few weeks at a new school, St Vincent's National School in Glasnevin. St Vincent's had a primary school and a secondary school. Jason had been going to a school in Finglas, but his mam thought he might like this school better. Jason liked St Vincent's because it had loads of sports.

He had to make new friends. He was also more vulnerable to slagging because he looked different to other kids.

He was the only kid with Asian heritage in his whole school. Some lads would slag him for 'looking Chinese'. Others would ask why he looked different. Either way, they made Jason very self-conscious.

He'd feel most awkward during lunch, when lads would head to the shop for sausage rolls. Jason just tried to keep his head down and blend in. But that was hard sometimes.

After lunch his teacher Mrs Morris made an announcement.

'Class, I'm delighted to say we're going to have a special guest,' she said. 'Actually, we're going to have two special guests. I'd like to introduce you to Joey Boylan, and his friend from America, Michael Tait. They're both involved in the basketball team here at St Vincent's.'

Joey and Michael entered the room. Michael was extremely tall. He had to bend his knees so he didn't hit his head on the door frame. The whole class gasped. They had never seen someone so tall in their lives.

'Hiya, everybody! My name is Joey. I'm here today to talk about the great sport of basketball.'

Joey was as Dublin as they come. He wore glasses and was in his twenties. Beside him, Michael looked like a giant. He was tall and athletic and had dark skin. He had an orange basketball in his hand.

Joey and Michael both wore a St Vincent's blue and yellow tracksuit.

'I'm the coach for the St Vincent's basketball team. We play in the Irish SuperLeague. I'm joined today by our star player. He comes from the United States of America. His name is Michael Tait. Everyone say hi to Michael.'

'Hi Michael!' everyone in the class said.

'Hi everybody, it's a real pleasure to meet you all,' Michael said.

'Does everybody know what Michael is holding in his hands?' Joey asked.

'It's a basketball!' Jason shouted. He was the first in with an answer.

'That's absolutely right, young man. This orange ball is a basketball. And I want to let you in on a little secret: with this orange basketball, you can play the greatest game in the whole wide world.'

Michael took the ball and placed it on his finger and began to spin it. Everybody in the class was amazed.

'If you've never played it, you should know it's a wonderful sport,' Michael said.

'St Vincent's have a very good team and we're

always on the lookout for exciting new players,' Joey said. 'Basketball is a brilliant sport that's easy to play. Whether you're a boy or a girl, whether you're white, black or purple, it doesn't matter! Everyone's welcome on the basketball court. And best of all, look outside, you see that?'

The class looked out the window. It was raining cats and dogs.

'Best of all, you don't have to be out playing in the wind and rain and muck. We play indoors.'

'And if you practise hard enough and you get lucky and you eat all your vegetables, you might even be good enough to play for Ireland someday,' Michael said.

'We're holding training sessions every Tuesday at the basketball hall here at the school. Please join us,' Joey said. 'And if you're up for it, Michael will give you a quick demonstration of the skills of the game.'

Michael dribbled the ball between his legs and around his back. He made it all look so easy.

Jason was starstruck. He had never seen anyone so tall and athletic in his entire life.

A few of Jason's classmates stood up and tried to measure themselves against Michael. Their heads barely passed his belt! Michael extended his hands as well. They were huge. He could hold the ball in the palm of his hand.

'Can you do a slam dunk?' Jason asked him.

'It's not my speciality,' Michael said. 'But I can dunk, yes.'

Jason didn't need to hear anything else. He needed to learn this sport.

'How do I become a basketball player?' Jason asked Joey after class.

'We'll teach you everything you need to know,' Joey said. 'Come down to training on Tuesday evenings.'

'OK, you can count on me,' Jason said.

For the rest of the school day, all Jason could think about was basketball.

When his mam came home from work that evening, Jason ran straight over to her and met her as she opened the door.

'Mam, we need to get a basketball hoop and a basketball for the house. Please!'

'Okay, Jason, we can look into it,' his mam said. 'First you need to let me take off my coat.'

'Pleeeeeeeeeeeeeease? I want to be a basketball

player,' Jason said.

'I'll see, I'll see' she said. Jason trusted his mam to find a solution.

When Jason came home the next day, there was a brand-new basketball waiting for him.

Jason hugged his mam so hard. He knew she'd do anything for him. He loved her so much. She was the best mam in the whole world.

Jason then set out to become the best basketball player in Finglas. It was going to be tough, but he knew he could do it. The first thing any basketball player would have to learn is how to dribble the ball.

On the road in the front of his house he practised bouncing the ball up and down with his right hand. Once his dribbling began to improve, he began to practise his shooting. There were no basketball hoops in the area so Jason would practise shooting at the electrical poles out on the street. There were numbers on them, about ten feet off the ground. Jason figured he'd just aim at them. It was better than nothing! The more he did it, the more accurate his shooting became. He grew more and more comfortable with the ball in his hands as well.

'How are you getting on with the basketball?' Uncle Eddie would ask.

'It's tough going, but I love it,' Jason said.

Jason knew if he was going to get better at basketball, he'd have to watch as much of the sport as possible. So he started watching NBA highlights on BBC on the weekends. The NBA was the American basketball league. The best of the best played in the NBA.

'Welcome to Boston Garden for the Boston Celtics vs the LA Lakers,' the American commentator would say and the camera would show a packed arena and thousands of screaming fans.

It was amazing to watch NBA players in action. They were acrobatic and incredibly athletic, but also they were so tall! There's one player he especially loved to watch. He was a young player with a bald head named Michael Jordan. He played for the Chicago Bulls. He could fly like a bird when he played. Jason learned so much about the sport from watching the Americans play.

And while the NBA was full of some of the tallest men Jason had ever seen in his life, it wasn't only tall players that succeeded in the NBA. There were a few really short players as well who were stars. One was named Spud Webb and he played for the Atlanta Hawks. Seeing Spud play in the NBA made Jason realise that anyone could play professional sports if they just tried hard enough.

Jason also got Uncle Brian and Uncle Eddie to bring him to St Vincents' matches in the Irish SuperLeague whenever they played a home match. It wasn't the NBA, but the games were really exciting. There were some really talented American players like Michael who were nearly good enough to play in the NBA.

Teams from Cork and Mayo and Belfast would travel to Dublin for games on Saturday nights in the winter. It might not have been on TV very often, but basketball was a big deal in Ireland.

'We've got a surprise for you, Jason,' Uncle Eddie said one day after Jason came home from school. 'Come out back.'

What could it be? Jason thought.

He ran out back and hanging from the door of the shed was a basketball hoop. Now Jason could really practise! Morning, noon and night, he was outside working on his jump shot or practising free throws or shooting lay-ups. It didn't matter if it was bucketing rain. There was no sweeter sound in the whole entire world than when he made a shot and the ball made that swish sound when it went through the net.

'I'm ready to join St Vincent's!' he told his uncles.

CHAPTER 7

A FIRST TASTE OF CROKE PARK

It was a very important day for Jason, and he had barely slept a wink the night before. Jason was now in sixth class and his school St Vincent's were playing in the Cumann na mBunscoil final in Croke Park.

Jason's whole week was filled up with sport. That week, he and his mam sat down to make a training calendar.

'It's hard to keep track of all your training,' she said.

'Okay,' Jason said. 'Well Monday and Wednesday, I have soccer training with Rivermount. We'd have a match on a Saturday then.'

Jason's mam made a note on the calendar.

'And then Tuesday and Thursday, I'm with St Vincent's. There'll be a game on the weekends as well.'

'And now on Fridays, I'm training with the St Vincent's Gaelic football team!' he said.

'You'll be flat out with sport,' Jason's mam said.

'I know, but I love it,' Jason said.

He barely had a free minute, but he had to make time in his schedule for the St Vincent's Gaelic football team. Kids his age didn't get many chances to lift silverware in Croke Park.

'I hear you're playing in Croke Park today,' his nan said at breakfast that morning.

'That's right, Nanny.'

'Don't forget that you're representing not only yourself and not only your school, but your whole family. Do us proud today, son,' she said with a big smile.

Jason was buzzing on the walk to school. His head was focused on how his school could play their best match of the year. He pictured himself slotting a point over the bar into Hill 16.

When Jason walked into the classroom, he could see all of his classmates were as nervous as he was.

'Are we going to win today or what, lads?' Jason shouted, just before his teacher Mr McKeever entered the classroom.

'Yes!' everyone shouted at once.

Someone needed to break the tension – and it worked! It was a great feeling. Jason had felt like an outsider when he started at the school, but now he was becoming part of the gang. This was entirely down to sport.

'How's everybody feeling ahead of the match?' Mr McKeever said. He was also their coach.

'Good,' the class answered in unison.

'Now, I know you all want to win the trophy today, but please respect your opponents. It's not about whether you win or lose, but how you play the game,' their teacher said.

'Yes, sir,' they all answered.

It was very hard to focus on the schoolbooks that morning. Before lunch, everyone took a break to make signs and banners supporting the St Vincent's team.

'We all have a job to do, lads.' Jason said. 'Even if

you're not playing. Your shouting and roaring will make a huge difference.'

Jason loved playing all sports, but he didn't consider himself a Gaelic footballer. In fact, he wasn't even a member of a GAA club. He was a natural goal-scorer on the soccer pitch. He loved playing basketball more than anything else. But his uncles had given him a love for Gaelic football and the Dublin team. He'd learned the rules of the sport playing with his schoolmates. He was pretty good at it.

And there were some great rewards that came with playing Gaelic football, like playing in Croke Park – one of the greatest stadiums in the whole wide world!

His school was just a few kilometres from Croke Park so the team packed into a van and headed for Croker. The classmates who'd be shouting them on followed behind.

As the van drove along the Royal Canal, Jason got his first glimpse of Croke Park. He'd been there for Dublin matches, but this was different.

'This must be what it is like to play for the Dubs,' Jason said to his friend Seán.

Jason suddenly felt something he had never experienced in his young sporting career: pressure. All their classmates would be in the stands, shouting them on. They couldn't head back to Glasnevin without the cup. Their opposition was Scoil Mhuire, another Dublin school. Winning would be tough.

The van parked outside Croke Park and a steward escorted the team to their dressing room. Jason got goosebumps when he caught a glimpse of the beautiful green pitch. They changed into the school's blue and yellow kit in the Croke Park dressing room. Jason loved every second of the build-up to the match. Playing basketball and football were great and everything, but every Irish sportsperson dreamt of playing at Croke Park. Today Jason and his classmates were living the dream.

Croke Park was empty except for the students from the two schools as the teams walked out on the pitch, but Jason didn't care. He imagined the whole stadium full of supporters, chanting his name. He got a rush when he heard all of his classmates screaming him and his team on.

Jason started at corner forward. It was his job to score the points and goals. It was a big responsibility! There was only one problem. The lads couldn't get him the ball. Jason did what he could, but he had no effect on the game. Meanwhile, Scoil Mhuire had some brilliant footballers. They took the lead. Jason tried his best every time he got the ball, but he couldn't make an impact. He was subbed off before full time. In the end, St Vincent's lost. Jason was heartbroken when the final whistle went.

'Maybe Gaelic football isn't for us,' he said to Seán as they walked off the pitch.

'It's still pretty cool to be here. What a place,' Seán said.

Jason surveyed the whole stadium. It was phenomenal.

'Lads don't be down about this, it's just one game,' Mr McKeever said. 'You've had the opportunity to play in Croke Park. How many people can say that?'

That immediately made Jason happy. It was a privilege to play in Croke Park, win or lose.

Jason hated losing, but he realised that day sometimes the experience was more important than the result.

CHAPTER 8

LEARNING FROM JOEY

'What's your favourite sport?' Uncle Brian said.

Jason thought hard about it. He was thirteen now and loved all sports, but there was only one answer.

'Basketball,' Jason said.

It wasn't as glamorous in Ireland as the other sports he played or watched on TV, but he loved the game. When he played, he felt he could express his true personality. When Jason had a basketball in his hands, he felt he could do the impossible. When he was playing basketball, he also received a lot less slagging for having an Asian background.

Jason had been slagged his whole life for the way he looked. He couldn't really talk about it to his family or teachers. But when he played basketball, he felt he could release that energy.

That night, Jason had training at the St Vincent's basketball hall in Glasnevin. They had a big game coming up with Coláiste Éanna, one of their big rivals from the southside of the city.

Joey was a big reason why Jason loved basketball. He was so passionate about basketball as well as being a great teacher of the game.

'See what I'm holding in my right hand here, lads,' Joey said, at the start of training. 'On a basketball court, you can do the impossible. I've seen men fly.'

Jason could listen to Joey talk about basketball all day long.

Jason had already made some great friends playing basketball. His best mate on the team was Gareth Widners. Gar came from a basketball family and his older brother David had been picked for the Leinster U15 basketball team. They'd play against the best players from Munster, Ulster and Connacht. The best of those players would be picked to play for Ireland. The Leinster players would get really nice training tops and everyone in their school would know these lads were elite athletes.

'Make me a promise, Gar,' Jason had said after seeing David in his Leinster U15 kit. 'By the time we're fifteen, we'll both be picked for the Leinster team.'

'I promise,' Gar said with a smile

'Let's shake on it,' Jason said, extending his hand.

Gar shook his hand.

It was a deal. Even though Jason was still learning the game, he believed he could do it. Joey made Jason believe in himself.

'If you work hard, lads, you can achieve anything,' Joey would say.

Joey was the main man at St Vincent's. Not only did he coach Jason's under-13 team, but he coached practically every age level at the club. Joey also captained the St Vincent's team in the National League. His whole life seemed dedicated to basketball.

There was a lot of excitement in the squad that night because of the game against Coláiste Éanna at the weekend. They had a player named Callaghan who was one of the best young basketball players in Ireland.

'Great energy here tonight, lads. We'll finish with some free throws,' Joey said. 'Jason, can we chat for two minutes afterwards?'

'Sure thing,' Jason said.

Jason had only been playing for St Vincent's for a few months, but he would do anything for his coach. No coach had ever seemed as invested in Jason's success before.

'You're some dynamo out there, Jason,' Joey said. 'I can see you're picking up the game quickly. What I love is your defence.'

'Thanks coach,' Jason said.

Joey had taught Jason the art of defence. It was all about intensity: getting in your man's face and becoming a total nuisance. Jason was a natural at it!

'The time when we don't have the ball is as important as the time when we have the ball,' Joey would say. 'If you can get into your man's face, and be a nuisance for the man with the ball, you're just as important on my team as someone who can dunk the ball.'

'We've a big game coming up at the weekend, Jay,' Joey said. 'Éanna are serious. They've got some great players. I have a plan to beat them though. And it involves you marking Callaghan.'

Jason wasn't ready for that news. Callaghan was

one of the best young players in the country. He was about a foot taller than Jason, too. But Jason didn't flinch. He had total faith in his coach.

'OK, I can handle that,' Jason said.

'Bring your energy and make life miserable for him, and we'll have a chance,' Joey said.

The game would be held at the Oblate Hall in Inchicore.

'Are you nervous about the match?' Jason's mam said on the day of the game.

'A little bit,' Jason said. 'But the selectors for the Leinster and Ireland schoolboy team will be at the game to see Callaghan play. It's a great opportunity to make an impression.'

'Good thinking!' she said.

Joey gave the pregame team talk. He explained to the starting five that Jason would be marking Callaghan.

'Lads, I'll tell you a phrase the Yanks use. They say "It's not about the size of the dog in the fight, it's about the fight in the dog." Let's show these Éanna lads that we want it more than them.'

Jason played the position of point guard. It was arguably the most important position on the court.

The point guard would dribble the ball up the court and set up the play. More importantly, they'd establish the tempo the team played at. Joey said it was like being the conductor in an orchestra. They made everything happen. It was the perfect position for Jason. He wasn't as big as the other lads. But he could read the game. Then, when the other team had the ball, he was relentless. He had so much energy.

'C'mon Jason let's show them how it's done,' Joey said, as Éanna brought the ball up the court for their first possession of the game.

Jason ran straight to Callaghan and put a hand on his chest.

'Make sure he knows you're there,' Joey shouted.

'Wasn't expecting a lad your size to be marking me,' Callaghan said, with a laugh.

'Big things come in small packages,' Jason said. He stood as close as he possibly could to Callaghan without knocking into him.

'Get so tight on him that you know the size of his jersey,' Joey had said before the game.

Jason tried to get that close.

The Éanna point guard fed the ball into Callaghan

at the top corner of the perimeter, with his back to the net. Jason knew Callaghan was right-handed. Jason defended to the left-hand side of the court, tempting Callaghan to play to his weak side.

Callaghan was unprepared for the intensity of Jason's defending. He picked up his dribble and the second he did, Jason pounced on him, flailing his arms left and right to prevent Callaghan from shooting or passing. Callaghan forced a pass towards the hoop, but Jason got a hand on it and St Vincent's turned the ball over. They raced down the court on a fast break, which Gar completed with a lay-up. Jason pumped his fist.

'Great work, Jason,' Joey hollered. 'That's because of you.'

Jason nodded. It turned out Joey was right again. It didn't matter how tall you were. If you had the hunger and the passion, you could make it as a basketball player.

CHAPTER 9

A SUMMER IN THE COUNTRY

Summer holidays had just begun. Jason was fourteen and he was in the car with Uncle Eddie. They were driving around beautiful north County Cork. The sun was splitting the rocks. The cows in the fields took cover in the shade beside the stone walls.

I'm an awful long way from home, Jason thought.

It was the most nervous, and most excited, Jason had felt in a long time. He hadn't said much on the drive down. That day, Jason was moving to Charleville with Uncle Eddie for the summer holidays. Uncle Eddie had taken a job in a meat factory in Charleville, a village in north Cork, about a half hour from Limerick, a few years ago. Since Jason had just finished his first year of secondary school, he was now old enough to spend the whole summer with Uncle Eddie.

'Listen, Jason, don't worry about these culchies,' Uncle Eddie said with a laugh. 'You'll love them by the time you leave.'

Uncle Eddie spoke in a thick Dublin accent. He'd be the last person you'd expect to encounter in a place as small as Charleville. Jason had visited him a few times and found that he loved the place.

Before the school year ended, he asked his mam and nan what they'd think of him going down for the whole summer.

'It'd be great fun,' Jason said.

Jason's mam wasn't so sure.

'It's an awful long way from home,' she said.

But his nan intervened.

'I think it could be the making of him,' his nan said. 'A few months down the country never did anyone any harm,' she said.

It was settled. Jason was going to Cork for the summer.

Jason had only lived in Finglas, and he was so excited to get to know a new part of the world. All he knew was city life – with traffic and estates and people everywhere. He was keen to see what it was like down the country.

'Did you bring a hurley down?' Uncle Eddie said.

'No I didn't,' Jason said.

'Not a bother,' he said. 'That's the first thing we'll sort out. There's training Tuesdays and Thursdays, just so you know. They're expecting you down.'

'But I've hardly hurled in my whole life,' Jason said.

'Then you'll have to learn!' Uncle Eddie said, with a laugh.

'Fair enough!' Jason said. He was up for the challenge.

Uncle Eddie had gotten involved with the hurling club in the town, who were known as Ballyhea.

As they drove, Uncle Eddie told him everything he knew about the Ballyhea hurling team. They wore black and white, and were known as the Magpies. They won their first and only Cork senior title way back in 1896. Eddie had gotten involved in managing Ballyhea's underage hurlers as soon as he moved down to Cork.

'The great thing about the GAA is how it gets

you involved in the whole community,' Uncle Eddie said, as they arrived in the town. 'You'll have loads of friends here in no time.'

The next morning there was a knock on the door.

Jason opened it and found five lads and a sheep-dog waiting at the doorstep.

'My mam said you'd moved down from Dublin. Are you up for a kickabout?' said a lad with red hair.

Jason looked back at Uncle Eddie for permission.

'Go on, son!' Uncle Eddie shouted from the kitchen.

'Deadly!' Jason said.

'My name is Diarmuid and these are my brothers, you'll learn their names eventually.'

They played a few games of headers and volleys, and three-v-three.

Jason was desperate to prove to these lads that he was a decent footballer. At one point during the three-a-side game, he tried a back-heel flick on Diarmuid and dribbled right past him. The lads were impressed.

Jason soon grew to love life in the country. He'd spend all of his afternoons having a kickabout with

the lads or roaming the fields. He ...
He'd train with the U14 hurlers twice ...
had a lot to learn in terms of stick w...
speed made him dangerous to mark.

He played his natural position: full forward

'Sport is just about who wants it more,' Uncle Eddie used to say and Jason knew if he hurled with hunger, he could make up for any limitations he had with a hurl while he learned the game.

When Jason wasn't training, he'd hang out with Diarmuid on his family farm. He'd help out when the cattle needed milking or the silage needed spreading. Everybody was laid back and funny. All of Diarmuid's family thought it was hilarious to have a kid from Dublin around the farm. He'd stay over at Diarmuid's many nights. It was like he was part of their family. Finglas felt a million miles away.

Jason knew he was really at home the first time he went to a Ballyhea hurling match with his Uncle Eddie. The Ballyhea pitch was small and the whole town must have turned out for the match, and they were so passionate about their club. The players wore the black and white shirt of the club with real pride. When Jason stood on the sidelines with his tes, he felt like he was part of the club.

He was a big Dublin GAA supporter, but Jason had never joined a club in the city. After a few weeks living in the country, Jason was proud to be a Ballyhea man.

CHAPTER 10

NORTH CORK GAELS

The weeks flew by that summer. He'd talk to his mam and nan on the phone on Sunday nights, but he'd didn't miss Dublin too much. With Uncle Eddie's instruction, Jason was quickly learning the game of hurling. Even though he was a novice at the sport, he'd cracked the starting team for the Ballyhea under-14s.

On the last Sunday in July, they had a huge match away to North Cork Gaels, a club just twenty minutes away.

'These local derbies are always fierce,' Uncle Eddie said.

Jason may not have been from Ballyhea, but he knew beating North Cork Gaels was so important.

The referee threw the ball in. There was a proper edge to this game. Hurls were swinging, elbows were flying.

'You're a long way from China,' said the North Cork Gaels lad marking him.

'OK, so this is how it's going to be,' Jason said to himself.

Jason wasn't going to let him away with that. He plastered his man with a hard shoulder.

He knocked the North Cork Gaels player over. He would have hit him harder if he could, but Jason didn't want to get a red card.

Jason expected that shoulder to shut his marker up. But the comments continued.

'Why don't you head back to the jungle?' the North Cork Gaels full back said in the second half. Jason had been listening to this abuse for the whole match and he'd finally had enough. He found it so hard to control his temper when people were saying hateful things.

Jason clattered his marker with his hurl in the ribs and wrestled him to the ground. He knew it was wrong, but he didn't care. What the North Cork Gaels player was saying was plain wrong. Jason needed to defend himself. He'd heard this abuse in Dublin. He thought he might be able to escape it down the country. Sadly, he was wrong.

Soon the referee was blowing his whistle in a panic and Jason's teammates were pulling him away. Jason tried to get as many punches in as possible. He didn't care anymore. He was sick of the abuse.

As things quietened down, he could hear Uncle Eddie shouting at him.

'Jason, Jason, you're off,' he roared. He could tell Uncle Eddie was not pleased.

'What are you at? You can't be swinging your hurl at people like that!' Uncle Eddie shouted.

Jason burst out crying.

'You don't understand what I have to put up with. What did I do to deserve this? I'm the same as everyone else here,' he shouted.

'You can't be down here if you're going to be carrying on like that. Either sort yourself out or head back to Finglas.'

Jason watched the rest of the match from the sidelines. He didn't care who won. He and Uncle Eddie didn't speak much on the drive home. Jason kept crying. He loved it in Cork, but he didn't want to stay if he wasn't welcome.

By the time he got home, he decided he'd had enough. He'd go back to Finglas. He grabbed his gear bag and began to fold his clothes.

As Jason was packing Diarmuid came into the room. Jason could see he was crying too.

'Eddie said you were heading back to Dublin,' Diarmuid said.

'Yeah I am. I'm sick of it,' Jason said

'Don't go back to Dublin,' Diarmuid said.

'You should have heard what those North Cork Gaels fellas were saying to me,' Jason said.

'Don't mind them. They're eejits. That's not what we're like down here,' Diarmuid said. 'All the lads from the team want you to stay as well. To be honest, we need you if we're going to win the north Cork championship this year.'

They both laughed and Jason stopped packing his clothes and the two of them headed over to Diarmuid's house. It meant so much to Jason to hear Diarmuid say those things. It meant even more to Jason to see how upset Diarmuid was at the idea that he might return to Dublin. He felt like crying tears of happiness now.

'Will you stay for tea, Jason?' Diarmuid's mam said. 'We're having fish fingers.'

'I'd say I would, yeah,' Jason said.

After everything that happened that day, Jason felt part of the family now.

After he finished his tea, Uncle Eddie called to the O'Riordans' to collect him.

'I lost my temper with you today, and I'm sorry,' Uncle Eddie said. 'I'm the coach for all these lads, not just you. I expect a higher standard from you. Because we're family.'

'I know,' Jason said.

'But those things that were said to you, it's not right,' Eddie said. 'I'm sorry you have to put up with that.'

'I've heard it my whole life,' Jason said.

'I understand, Eddie,' Jason said.

They shook hands. Jason knew his uncle wanted the best for him. It was funny: it was horrible to be on the receiving end of that abuse, but Jason felt much better for finally speaking out about it. There was a word for it: racism. Jason knew the only way this abuse was going to stop was by people speaking up about it.

CHAPTER II

SOCCER STAR

After the summer ended, Jason came back to Dublin. Jason was fourteen. He was a teenager now. Everything was changing. The world seemed so much bigger now. He'd still jump on the bus to Cork and visit Uncle Eddie on the odd weekend, especially if the Ballyhea hurlers needed him. But he was starting to look to the future.

'What sort of job would you like when you're a grown-up?' Jason's mam asked over dinner one night.

'I want to play sport for a living,' he told his mam.

'I know, Jason,' she said. 'And that's a great dream to have, but you need to have alternatives lined up in case it doesn't work out.'

Jason wasn't convinced. He just thought he needed to work harder at playing sport.

Most young lads in Ireland dreamed of playing football with Liverpool or Manchester United, depending on who you supported. Talented footballers around his age were being scouted by big English clubs. He knew of a few lads from Rivermount who'd gone over to England and join the academies of First Division clubs.

His mate Darren had been back and forth between Dublin and London because Tottenham Hotspur had been interested in signing him.

Then there was Pat Fenlon, who started out with Rivermount and went to Chelsea for a few years. He signed with St Patrick's Athletic and was one of the best players in the League of Ireland.

One day, Jason received a call from Jimmy, a coach with St Kevin's Boys, one of the most famous youth football clubs in Dublin.

'Jason, we've seen great things from you with Rivermount. We'd like you to join us.'

'That's brilliant,' Jason said. 'But I'll need to discuss it with my family.'

Founded in 1959, St Kevin's Boys was one of

Dublin's biggest clubs. This was a serious football club and playing for them would take a lot of Jason's time.

That night he chatted to his mam and Uncle Brian about it.

'It'd be a great opportunity to put yourself against the best lads in Dublin,' Uncle Brian said.

'It sounds like a big commitment. Do you think you'd have enough time with basketball and hurling?' his mam asked.

'I know. I'd be very busy. But I think it would be worth it.'

Jason knew he was at a pivotal age in his development as a footballer.

'Would you be open to going to England?' Uncle Brian asked.

'I'd be open to anything!' Jason said.

'It's a difficult life over there, just to warn you,' Uncle Brian said. 'You'd be living in digs in London or Manchester.'

'But it would be worth it to walk out of the tunnel at Anfield and hear "You'll Never Walk Alone,"' he said.

'It's true.'

'What do you think, Mam?'

'Listen to your heart, Jason,' she said. 'If you really want to do this, that's great. Just be ready to make the time commitment.'

Jason liked the idea of playing for St Kevin's Boys. He said yes. They played him on the wing and, that year, Jason played a huge part in helping them get to the SFAI Cup final. The best schoolboy teams in Ireland vied for this trophy. The final pitted them against the Munster champions Carrigaline.

Amazingly, the Cup final was at Tolka Valley Park, just a stone's throw from home. All his family came down to watch him. Some of his mates from the basketball team joined as well.

'What's the main difference between football and basketball?' Uncle Brian had asked the night before the match.

It was a good question. Jason thought about it for a few moments. Jason used his speed to his advantage in both sports.

'When I play basketball, I feel more creative,' Jason said. 'On the football pitch, I feel like I need to be more aggressive.'

Since joining St Kevin's Boys, Jason found himself up against bigger defenders who weren't afraid to kick at his ankles to slow him down. They could see how fast Jason was, and sometimes a kick was the only way to slow him down.

'Sometimes you have to fight fire with fire,' Jason would tell himself, and he was never afraid to throw his whole body into a challenge. It meant he played on the edge. Referees always seemed to have an eye on him. But there was no point being shy.

Carrigaline were a decent side, but St Kevin's Boys were a different animal. With all of his friends and family gathered on the sideline, Jason was determined to put in a big performance. In the first half, one of his midfielders played a beautiful ball into space, on the edge of the penalty box. Jason beat his man and slotted the ball past the keeper.

Goal Sherlock!

Jason added an assist to his tally and St Kevin's Boys won the final 3-1.

As Jason celebrated with his friends, he was approached by one of the organisers of the tournament.

'Congratulations Jason, you've been named Man of the Match,' he said, handing Jason a medal. 'Well done son. You played brilliantly.'

Jason now had two medals around his neck. Nothing made him happy quite like sport.

CHAPTER 12

THE BIG GAME

t was an exciting time for Jason and his family. Jason's mam had met her future husband. His name was Bill. He was a lovely guy who loved sport. Jason got on great with him. They all moved into Bill's house, about ten-minute's drive from Carrigallen Park.

Jason was also going places on the basketball court. He'd been selected for the Irish national team. Their first game was England, the old enemy! He could hardly believe it. He'd never known pressure like this.

The games took place in the De La Salle basketball hall in Castlebar County Mayo. It was the first night of the Four Nations under-15 basketball tournament. The best young basketball players in Ireland, England, Scotland and Wales would be going up against each other to see which country was the best.

Jason was really nervous.

Luckily, Joey was a coach with the team.

'Keep calm out there, lads. Treat it like an ordinary game of basketball,' Joey said in the dressing room, ten minutes before tip off.

That's good advice, Jason thought. Then he closed his eyes and heard the noise from the spectators. How could he keep calm? This was Ireland against England! And he was right in the middle of it!

Jason felt so lucky to be part of this team. A few months ago, he and Gar had been invited to play for the Leinster U15 team. The lads celebrated wildly when they got the news. They'd made a promise to each other when they were thirteen and they kept it.

And while it was great playing for Leinster and wearing the Leinster kit, Jason and Gar quickly realised there was a bigger prize at stake. If they did well for Leinster, they might get selected to play for Ireland. And so they worked even harder.

And then one day the letter arrived in the post, inviting Jason to play for the Ireland team. Gar received the same letter.

'After tonight, we'll be Ireland internationals,' Gar said in the dressing room.

'We can't let the country down!' Jason said.

When Jason received his Ireland kit, it was the proudest day of his life. The jersey and the shorts were green with white trim. There was a shamrock over the right shoulder and a number over the heart. They also were given silky white warm-up tops, just like professional basketballers. Jason was given number 10.

'To represent your country is the greatest honour of any sportsperson, professional or amateur,' Uncle Brian said.

The team met up to train a few times before the tournament to train. There were lads from Cork and Belfast and Mayo and Dublin. They all had different accents but they all loved basketball and they were all Irish.

'I feel so lucky to be on this team,' Jason said to Uncle Brian.

The team would stay in a hotel in Castlebar for

the weekend. They wore a shirt and tie to the game, just like professional athletes.

'Lads, before we head out there, I just want one word with you,' Joey said. 'Those English boys are good. They're big, they're skillful. And if you beat them tonight, you'll do what no other Irish team has done before. No Irish boys' team has ever beaten England before in a game of basketball. Can you believe that? That changes tonight. Now come on, lads, put your hands in the middle.'

Jason and his teammates gathered in a circle and each put a hand into the middle. They'd seen NBA teams do this before games so they thought they'd do it as well.

'On three, we say "team",' Joey said. 'One ... two ... three.'

'TEAM!' they all shouted.

Jason and his teammates sprinted out of the dressing room. They arrived into an atmosphere that they had never experienced in their young careers. The noise was deafening. It was like the whole town of Castlebar – scratch that, the whole county of Mayo! – had packed into the small sports hall to watch Ireland play England. Jason knew his whole family were out in the stands cheering him on, but he tried to stay focused on what was happening on the court.

'You nervous?' Jason said to Gar, as they stood on the lay-up line.

'Big time!' Gar said with a laugh.

Jason was so happy to have his good friend Gar and his favourite coach Joey with him. Jason noticed a group of girls sitting behind the Ireland bench. And soon as he noticed them, he made himself concentrate on the game. Jason had never known attention like this!

The teams lined up along the half court line for the national anthems. When 'God Save The Queen' was played, the sports hall fell silent and Jason thought about how badly he wanted to win this game. When '*Amhrán na bhFiann*' was played, he sang with all of his heart. He was so proud to be Irish.

Joey had picked Jason to start the game at point guard. It was up to Jason to control the pace of the game and implement Joey's game plan. If Ireland were going to have any chance against these English lads, Jason knew he'd have to play a huge game.

Jason took a second to look at the English team as they finished their warm-ups. They had brown skin, they had black skin, they had white skin. But they were all big and they could play.

Jason decided he needed to make an impact on the game early. England won the tip-off and controlled the ball. The English point guard brought the ball up the court slowly and a bit carelessly, and Jason saw an opportunity and stole the ball away! The crowd rose to its feet and cheered for Jason. The English players hadn't been expecting it. Even though it was just one play in the game, England suddenly realised that Ireland were no pushovers. The Boys in Green were here to play.

Jason took that confidence and he built on it. Ireland built up a lead and they didn't look back. When the final buzzer sounded, Ireland had won by nine points. The hall erupted with noise and the Ireland team celebrated as if they'd won the World Cup final.

Jason sought out Gareth and they bear hugged each other. Then they met Joey and embraced.

'Well done, Jason,' Joey said. 'Not bad for a few lads from Finglas.'

Jason had never known a feeling like this before. Sure, it was great to be invited to represent Ireland and wear the green jersey, but to win the biggest game of his life – against England of all teams! – was a whole new level of happiness.

And even more importantly, Jason was a vital player for the team. They couldn't have beaten England without him. It was a rush of energy, like eating a thousand sweets at once. When he was celebrating with his teammates, Jason no longer felt different. He belonged.

As he closed his eyes and tried to sleep that night, all he could hear were the Castlebar fans shouting 'Ireland! Ireland! Ireland!' He wanted that feeling to go on forever.

CHAPTER 13

WEST HAM

'Ladies and gentlemen, we'll be landing in Dublin in ten minutes, please fasten your seat belts.'

Jason was on an Aer Lingus flight to Dublin from London. As the plane landed, he looked out the window at all the estates of north Dublin. He saw a few football pitches and it made him happy. It felt good to be home.

Jason hadn't seen his family for the whole weekend. He was sixteen and it was a long time to be away from home. He knew they'd all be at the airport to collect him. His mam said even his nan was going to come. Jason had flown to London with his old buddy and teammate Pato. He was excited to see them all, but he knew they'd have a lot of questions as well.

That weekend, Jason had flown to London for a trial with West Ham Football Club. West Ham were an English First Division club that was based in east London and had a great history.

Jason had been spotted by a scout for West Ham named Shay; West Ham were on the lookout for the next great Irish footballer. The club invited him to London for a weekend for a trial. Shay paid a visit to Jason's house to explain why West Ham was a great club for a young fella to join. This was serious.

'Welcome to London,' said Jimmy, the man from the West Ham academy who gave them a tour of the club. He had the thickest English accent Jason had ever heard. Jimmy was their guide for the weekend.

West Ham had some decent footballers. They played in Upton Park. Jimmy gave them a tour of Upton Park and the academy. He showed them all the facilities and took them to West Ham's match that weekend, which was an FA Cup tie.

They also trained for a day with the West Ham first team. The English lads were all good football-ers, but Jason held his own.

'You're a fine footballer, Jason,' said a man named Martin who was head of the academy. 'You've got a real future in the game.'

'Thank you, sir,' Jason said.

Overall, it was a brilliant experience. Now Jason just had to decide whether he wanted to go back.

★ ★ ★

Jason collected his sports bag from the carousel and then hurried through customs. His mam and nan and Bill were waiting for him. Jason sprinted over to them and gave them a big hug.

'We missed you,' his mam said.

'I missed you, too,' Jason said.

'Tell us about it in the car,' Bill said.

'I will, I will!' Jason said.

And when he got into the car, he told them everything he could remember.

About how they were taken for fish and chips, and how they were given a lift in an old London black cab, and how the people at the club said things you'd only hear English people say on TV like 'Alright guv'nor'. And he talked about how he got to meet the West Ham team and how angry their supporters were when they conceded a late goal. Jason talked the whole way home.

His family loved hearing all his news.

'It sounds really exciting,' Jason's mam said.

'Did you like it, Jason? It sounds like you did,' his nan asked.

'Well, I don't know,' he said. 'It was great to visit, but I don't know if I'd like to stay.'

Jason knew if he took an offer to play with a team like West Ham, he'd have to leave school and move to London on his own. He'd have to live with a family he didn't know. And here was no guarantee he'd get a professional contract at the end of it.

As Jason went to bed that night, all he could think about was seeing his mates in St Vincent's the next day. He'd be gutted to leave Dublin for London.

When he woke up the next morning, Jason was delighted to be in his own bed.

The life of an English footballer was nice and

all, but nothing beat being at home.

CHAPTER 14

THE HOME OF BASKETBALL

Jason stood in a queue at Dublin Airport with a few of his Ireland teammates. He had a ticket for an Aer Lingus flight in his hand. Joey was checking the departures board.

'Gate 313. Dublin to JFK,' he said. 'Next stop: the Big Apple.'

Jason was going to the home of basketball. New York City, USA.

Joey was taking Jason and a group of the best players from the Irish team to the States for a month. They'd fly into New York, but their final destination was a place called the Poconos Mountains. They'd be attending the longest running basketball camp in America. There, for the next four weeks,

Jason would play basketball against America's best young basketball players.

'You'll be up against future NBA players here,' Joey said. 'There'll be a few coaches from the big universities as well.'

'Hopefully I can make a good impression,' Jason said. He knew the odds were against him, but Jason hadn't given up on his dream of playing basketball in America.

That year, Jason had been voted as the best young basketball player in Ireland. He'd travelled all around Europe with Joey and the Ireland team. The sport had been the making of him. This camp would help Jason decide if he would take the next step with his basketball career, and move to America.

Joey brought the best young Irish players in the country to this camp every year. It was an amazing opportunity, but it also made Jason a little nervous.

'How good are these American lads, really?' Jason asked Joey on the plane. 'Are they going to embarrass us?'

'Don't worry about that,' Joey said. 'It's the same game wherever you go in the world. It's just a ball and a hoop. You wouldn't be going to this camp if you didn't belong.'

That made Jason feel more confident.

'Do you think one of us Irish lads could make the NBA?' he asked Joey once. Everyone dreamed of playing in the NBA, but it was so hard for an Irish kid to make it.

There would be university scouts at this camp on the lookout for promising young players. A few of the best Irish players had gone to the USA on basketball scholarships.

'American universities would be interested in you. It could be an option for you, Jason, if you were really serious about it,' Joey said.

Before flying over to the camp, he'd talked to Uncle Eddie about it all.

'The thing you'd have to decide Jason is whether you'd want to give everything else up so you could just concentrate on basketball.'

'I know,' Jason said.

'If you were to go to America for university to play, it would mean no time for football. And you'll struggle to find a game of hurling over there,' he said with a laugh.

The flight to America was so long. But it was fun

to watch a movie on a plane and daydream about what America would be like. Jason had a window seat, and when the plane got close to New York, he could see all the skyscrapers and the Statue of Liberty. He'd only seen them in movies before. It was amazing.

The drive from JFK Airport to the Poconos was long, but Jason didn't mind. Everything was bigger in America: the cars, the motorways, the hamburgers! At the Poconos camp, everything was bigger again. The gym they trained in was massive. The American players were pretty big, as well! There were black kids and white kids and they all played like they'd been given basketballs for birthday presents when they were babies.

But Jason found that once it was time to play basketball, he was just as good as these American lads. Jason played the game with fire in his belly. He wanted to prove he belonged.

Amazingly, all the American lads treated him like an ordinary American kid. They presumed he was Asian-American.

All the American kids called all of the Irish players 'Irish', but they called Jason by his first name.

They'd say: 'you play some tough D, Jay', when they wanted to complement his defence. Or 'you've got some serious jets, Jay', after he'd track down a loose ball that was scurrying out of bounds.

They might have Air Jordan basketball shoes on their feet, but he had as much fight as any of them. Jason was named to the camp's All-Star team both weeks at the camp. It was a nice achievement.

After he won his award for the second time, he was approached by a coach as he was talking to Joey.

'You're a fantastic player, Jason,' the man said. 'My name is Coach Michael. I coach basketball at a high school not far from here. Your coach Joey tells me you come from Ireland.'

Michael said Ireland in a real funny and slow way, like it was pronounced 'Eye -RRRRR- land'.

'Michael coaches at a school in New York City, Jason,' Joey said.

'That's right,' Jason said. 'I'm actually the Irish schoolboy player of the year.'

'I'm not surprised,' Michael said. 'We're always on the lookout for talented players, and you're one of the best players at this camp. If you were interested in coming to America to play basketball, we'd be honoured if you'd join our team.'

'I'd have to think about it and discuss it with my family,' Jason said.

'Of course, of course. No pressure at all, just do me a favour and consider it, would you?' Coach Michael said.

'Sure thing,' Jason said.

It was an amazing opportunity, Jason thought. On one level, he loved it here, playing basketball every day. Basketball was a small sport in Ireland. In America, it was like a religion.

But that had its downsides too.

There were a hundred kids at this camp who were all at Jason's level. But America was a country of 300 million people. Meanwhile NBA teams only had twelve men on their rosters. Those NBA players weren't just the best of the best. They were the best of the best of the best. Playing in the Poconos made Jason love the game more. But it also made him more realistic about his future in the game.

'You've done well out here, Jason,' Joey said afterwards. 'There's scouts out here who are interested in you. If you wanted to go to a small college in America on a basketball scholarship, I'm sure we could make it happen.'

'Really?' Jason said.

'Absolutely,' Joey said.

'Now you'd be a long way from home, but it would be an adventure.'

'I can imagine,' Jason said.

'Where do you stand on all of it?' Joey asked.

Jason thought for a second.

'Here's what I think,' Jason said. 'I love basketball. But I don't love it enough to give everything else up.'

'That makes sense,' Joey said.

'And I'd miss my mam and nan. And I'd miss Dublin,' Jason said. 'I just want to play every sport.'

'That's fair enough, Jay. Do what you love, listen to your heart.'

On the last night of the camp, Joey took the Irish lads to the local McDonald's. They wanted to compare how the food at this McDonald's compared to the McDonald's in Phibsboro.

Jason had a Big Mac and fries.

'You know what, lads?' Jason said. 'I think I prefer the McDonald's back home.'

'What's the difference?' Joey said. 'Is it not the

exact same food?'

'I don't know,' Jason said. 'Everything's just a bit nicer back in Dublin. Do you know what I mean?'

Joey laughed.

'I do, I do,' he said.

CHAPTER 15

A BREAKTHROUGH IN BLUE

Jason was in the St Vincent's dressing room, putting on the school's kit. The St Vincent's senior Gaelic football team had a match against St David's, a school in Artane, across the northside of Dublin. Jason was in sixth year and today, he was starting at corner forward for St Vincent's.

Gaelic football was a bit of a laugh for Jason. It was a way to bond with his classmates. Jason loved playing any sport, so it goes without saying he loved Gaelic football. But so much of his time was given over to basketball with St Vincent's and football with St Kevin's Boys – plus the odd game with Ballyhea down in Cork – it meant that he never really had the time to play Gaelic football.

'When are you going to join us in Na Fianna, Jay?' said Seanie, one of the lads on the team.

A lot of the kids on the St Vincent's team played for the nearby GAA club, Na Fianna. They were always trying to recruit Jason. They knew he was getting trials with Premiership clubs.

'I can't, mate,' Jason said. 'I'm too busy!'

It was a tempting offer. Dessie Farrell, one of the best young footballers with Dublin, was a Na Fianna man. Dessie had been a few years ahead of Jason in St Vincent's, and he was one of Jason's favourite athletes. But even if Jason wanted to play more Gaelic football, Jason couldn't join a GAA club in Dublin because he was still a member of Ballyhea in Cork.

For Jason, Gaelic football was just a bit of craic. He didn't find the same kind of freedom when he played other sports. In basketball, players did slam dunks and behind-the-back passes. In hurling, players scored from a sideline cut. In soccer, strikers scored with rabonas and played back heels. Gaelic football was very traditional. Expression wasn't encouraged. So Jason didn't take these schools' games too seriously. His mate Gar and a few of the other lads from the basketball team were involved with the St Vincent's footballers.

His coach, Mr Horan, who was a science teacher in the school, had always believed in Jason's talent. He'd added Jason to the sixth year's team when he was only in second year.

'St David's are a serious outfit,' Mr Horan said before the game. 'You're going to have to put up a real fight today.'

'And remember, forwards,' Mr Horan said, before looking directly at Jason. 'Take your points and the goal will come.'

He was always hearing this old adage from Gaelic football coaches; Mr Horan was telling the lads to take the easy score instead of trying for the outrageous goal. Jason thought players should aim for the extraordinary, to do things that entertained the spectators. But the coaches like Mr Horan knew what was needed to win matches.

Jason wanted to put on a show against these lads from Artane. St David's put it up to St Vincent's, but Jason did his best for the team. He realised quickly he could beat his man for pace and finished the match with 1-4 to his name.

As soon as the full-time whistle blew, the St David

goalie ran straight to Jason.

'Well played, lad, well played,' he said to Jason, patting him on the back.

A few other St David's players nodded at him out of respect. Jason was surprised by all the attention. He was just having fun.

Then his art teacher Mr Whelan ran up to him.

'You were sensational out there today, Jason. Good man,' Mr Whelan said.

'No problem, thanks sir,' Jason said. He didn't know what to say. He wasn't used to all this praise.

'Apparently, the Dublin minor manager was there today,' Gar said, back in the dressing room after the game.

'Really?' Jason said.

'Don't think he'll be searching me out anyway!' Gar said, with a laugh. 'But you had a decent audition.'

'Do ya think?' Jason said. To him there was nothing special about it.

Jason showered and headed home. He was already thinking about his next basketball game. In school the next day, Mr Horan shouted after him as he walked down the hall.

'Jason!' he said. He sounded like he had urgent news – good news! – but urgent news.

'I got a phone call last night from Brian Talty. He's the manager of the Dublin minor footballers.'

'OK,' Jason said.

'He was at the St David's match yesterday. There's a trial for the Dublin minors next weekend. He wants you to attend.'

Jason thought this must be a joke.

'Are you sure – is this a stitch-up?' Jason said.

'Absolutely not,' Mr Horan said. 'They loved what they saw from you. They think you might be good enough for the minors.'

'But I'm not a Gaelic football player!' Jason said.

It was clear Mr Horan wasn't trying to wind him up.

'I have to think about it,' Jason said.

Jason didn't know what to think. On one level, he was honoured. He loved the Dublin jersey and the Dublin team. But he had no real experience playing Gaelic football. And he was already pretty busy with sport!

That evening, before dinner, he sat down with his mam and nan and Bill.

'I need your advice, everyone. They want me to do a trial for the Dublin minor footballers.'

'What's the problem?' Bill asked. 'This is amazing news.'

'How will he juggle it with everything else?' Jason's mam said.

'Exactly,' Jason said. 'My weeks are full enough as it is.'

'Well, how much time would be involved?' his nan asked.

'Training two nights a week, plus matches on the weekend in the summer if we can stay in the Leinster championship.'

'That's an awful lot,' his mam said.

'And what does your heart tell you?' Jason's nan asked.

Jason hadn't thought of that. He thought of himself walking onto the pitch at Croke Park wearing the blue shirt of Dublin. The thought of it gave him goosebumps.

'I guess I'd like to do it, but I'd want to give everything to it.'

'That's the right approach,' Bill said.

'It might mean less basketball and less football for

a year,' his mam said. 'But you can always go back to them. It's only one year.'

'There you go Jason. Always listen to your heart,' his nan said.

The first thing Jason did the next morning was head to Mr Horan's class to tell him the news.

'Mr Horan, let the selectors know I'll be there on Saturday.'

'*Maith thú*,' said Mr Horan. 'Good man yourself.'

The following Saturday, Jason got a lift out to the GAA pitches in Westmanstown, on the outskirts of County Dublin for the trial with the Dublin minors. Jason decided he wasn't going to take it too seriously. He knew the odds were stacked against him. So he'd invited some mates over the previous night to watch some movies on TV. They'd stayed up later than Jason planned and he was a bit tired.

As he stretched, Jason looked around for a familiar face.

'I don't know anyone here,' he said to himself.

And it was no wonder. While Jason was hurling down in the north Cork championship or going on trial for West Ham, these boys were honing their craft as Gaelic footballers. He could see the hunger on their faces to represent the Boys in Blue.

The lads were split into two groups and they played a game of As against Bs. Jason was with the Bs. He was thrown in the full forward line. The selectors stood in the stands with clipboards in their hands. Jason had been very casual about the whole process, but all of a sudden, things got very serious.

How many chances would he get to make the Dublin football team? He couldn't bottle this opportunity! But as the game went on, he started to panic. He needed a clean ball to make a difference, but his teammates in midfield kept missing him with their passes. Finally, one of the half backs found Jason clear of his marker. Jason had the ball in space. He was determined to show his ability and show his skill on the ball. Jason threw his marker a little shimmy and was ready to blast towards goal. But after taking three steps, Jason soloed the ball off his toe and just beyond his grasp. His marker picked up the loose ball and booted it away.

Jason put his hands on head.

'Not my day,' Jason said.

As the other team planned a substitution, the referee approached.

'Son, you're trying too hard. Don't panic. It's just a game.'

'Thanks, sir,' Jason said.

All of a sudden, Jason settled down. The next time the ball came to him, Jason tried to only do the simple thing, whether it was a fisted pass to an open man or a solo backwards to reset the attack. Slowly, Jason found himself right in the middle of the attack. Late in the second half, he peeled off his man, took a pass at the top of the parallelogram, and shot for goal. A point!

By the time the session was over, Jason was much happier with his performance. He might not have been the world's most polished Gaelic footballer, but he gave a decent account of himself.

That evening, he got a phone call from a selector inviting him to another trial next weekend.

And as the squad was whittled down over the following weeks, Jason kept expecting a call telling him 'thanks, but no thanks'. But it never came.

Instead when the phone call from the selector came, he would say, 'Jason congratulations, we'd like to see you at our next trial next Saturday.'

Then after a month of games with the best young

footballers in the capital, Jason received a phone call from the manager himself.

'Jason this is Alan Larkin. We want you to join the Dublin minors.'

Jason put the phone down and ran over to his mam and nan. They all hugged. They were so happy for him. All of a sudden, out of the blue, Jason was a Gaelic footballer.

'You'll be playing in front of Hill 16 this summer!' Uncle Brian said.

'Happy days!' Jason said.

He had to pinch himself. He couldn't believe this was happening.

CHAPTER 16

LEAVING CERT TIME

It was a very anxious time for Jason and his mates. It was the first day of the Leaving Cert. Jason took his seat at his desk.

'How do you feel?' Gar asked as they met outside school that morning.

'Can't wait to get this over with!' Jason said.

Jason was ready for the exam, but he was also excited to be done with it all. The World Cup was about to kick off and Ireland had qualified again! The Dublin minors were in the Leinster semifinal. This was sure to be a summer to remember.

Most of his mates had been fully preoccupied with the Leaving Cert over the last few months. On top of that, and his other sporting commitments,

Jason was on the Dublin minor team.

'Jason, how are your studies going?' his nan asked one evening after training.

'Fine now, Nanny,' Jason said.

'Don't neglect your books,' she'd say. 'You'll need something to fall back on if sport doesn't work out for you.'

'Thanks, Nanny,' Jason said. He knew she was probably right, but reading *Macbeth* or studying trigonometry was nowhere as exciting as playing sport. Now that Jason was in the exam hall of St Vincent's, he could tell people respected him. Things had changed a lot since first year. That was all because of sport.

Jason knew he should be thinking more about his English paper, but he kept thinking about Gaelic football. He was training two nights a week with the Dublin minors. That month, he transferred from Ballyhea. He needed to do it to play for Dublin.

'Mam and Nanny, I've decided to join Na Fianna,' Jason said.

'That's great, Jason,' his nan said. 'They're a fine club.'

Now Jason was training with the Na Fianna

senior team and the Dublin minor team. He wasn't a natural Gaelic footballer by any means, but with every training session, Jason felt more comfortable. His teammates with the minors were serious footballers. There was Ciaran 'Whelo' Whelan from Raheny in the midfield and Ray 'Cossie' Cosgrove from Kilmacud in the forwards with him. Jason could tell from one training session that they were going to be future Dublin stars.

Jason was less sure about his own abilities. He was selected as the starting corner forward in Dublin's first Leinster championship game of the year, against Kilkenny on the last day of April. It was a routine victory 0-19 to 0-07, but Jason didn't score. This annoyed him.

After the match, his manager Brian grabbed Jason for a quick chat.

'Don't force it, Jason,' he said. 'Let the game come to you. Your chances will come.'

It was frustrating for Jason because he knew once he got a sniff at goal, few defenders could stop him.

They were up against Kildare in the Leinster quarterfinal in Newbridge two weeks later.

Uncle Eddie came from Cork to watch him.

'Remember Jason, there's more than one way to skin a cat,' Uncle Eddie had told him before the match. What he meant was: even if he wasn't scoring himself, he could help his fellow forwards score.

Early on Jason got a sense that he had the beating of his defender. He won a free, which his teammate Eamon converted. He won four more frees, which were converted into points. Jason added a point himself. Now he was making an impact! Dublin eased in to the Leinster semifinal beating Kildare 2-11 to 1-07.

There was a gap of six weeks until they'd play Carlow in the Leinster semifinal, which gave him time to finish the Leaving Cert. That match would be in Croke Park, and it was far more exciting to daydream about than taking an English exam.

And when the Leaving Cert was all said and done, it was a bittersweet feeling. He'd never be back in St Vincent's as a student. The big world awaited him. It was exciting and a little bit terrifying. Everyone was swept up in World Cup fever again. It was a crazy World Cup – Ireland were in it, but England weren't! Paul McGrath put in a performance for the ages and Ray Houghton volleyed past Gianluca

Pagliuca as Ireland beat Italy 1-0 in their first game. The rest of the World Cup was pretty poor from an Irish perspective, but there was great excitement all the same.

A few weeks later, he jogged onto the Croke Park pitch for the first time since those Cumann na mBunscoil matches for a Leinster semifinal against Carlow.

'I never thought I'd be back playing here,' he told Whelo.

'You'll be grand,' Whelo said.

The match was a curtain-raiser for the Dublin seniors who were playing Louth in the Leinster semifinals. Croke Park was pretty empty as the game threw in. Jason could see his own mates from the St Vincent's basketball team in the stands. He tried not to make eye contact with them.

'C'mon Jayo, pull up your socks!' Gar shouted.

Jason tried to ignore him, but he knew all of his mates were in stitches.

Dublin were far superior to Carlow on the day. As Dublin built a lead, Jason felt entitled to flash some of his footballing style. Eamon played a hard pass into him, and Jason played the ball on the ground, like he was back with St Kevin's Boys, before rocketing a shot off the side of his boot and into the goal.

'What a hit!' Eamon shouted.

Jason couldn't believe it himself.

Dublin won with ease, 1-19 to 0-05. The Dublin seniors won that day as well, and it was all set to be a Leinster final day to remember in the capital.

The next day, Uncle Brian ran into the house with a copy of the newspaper under his arm.

'Wait until you read this lads!' he said.

He opened up the paper.

'This is Con Houlihan, Ireland's greatest sportswriter, writing in today's *Evening Press*: "I must single out the performance of Jason Sherlock of Dublin who scored a goal worthy of the 1994 World Cup in yesterday's minor semifinal."'

Jason grabbed the paper and read it himself. It seemed like people were beginning to notice him.

CHAPTER 17

THE POWER OF THE HILL

It was a huge day for Gaelic football in the nation's capital. Both the Dublin minors and the Dublin seniors were playing in the Leinster final that day. All of the newspapers were focused on the senior final between the Dubs and their great rivals Meath.

'Are you ready Jason?' his mam asked, knocking on his bedroom door. 'The breakfast is nearly ready.'

'I think so,' he answered. In truth he'd been up since 6am thinking about the match.

It was the biggest day of Jason's sporting career. As he put on his Dublin training top, he took a moment to look at his uniform. The shirt was sponsored by Arnotts, the famous department store. The jersey was light blue, with a dark blue collar. Over the right shoulder was a small 'g', which meant 'Guaranteed Irish'. The words *'Áth Cliath'* appeared over the crest, which featured three castles burning. Those castles appeared on the ancient coat of arms of Dublin.

Jason cherished the jersey and everything printed on it. He loved that the minors and the seniors wore the same kit. They were all part of one family.

The minor final would be played first. Dublin would play Wexford.

Jason had spent the day before the game reading previews of the game in the newspapers. All the articles talked about how it would be a sell-out crowd and how the Dubs would need a big lift from their supporters on Hill 16 to win the Leinster final. Jason had stood in Hill 16 for the All-Ireland when he was just a kid. He had never experienced 'the Hill' as a player. He hoped he might get a lift from it today.

As Jason and his teammates went through their warm-ups, he could tell today was going to be a lot different to his last match at Croker. The atmosphere was building early on. Most importantly,

Hill 16 was filling up. Jason remembered his days standing on his Uncle Brian's shoulders on the Hill. Now the supporters were shouting him on. It felt like yesterday!

Jason was named as Dublin's starting corner forward. It was his job to keep the scoreboard ticking over.

It was the toughest game Dublin had been in for the whole Leinster championship. Wexford were hungry. Dublin played into Hill 16 for the first half. The Hill gave them a great energy boost. But in the second half, with the game still in the melting pot, Dublin attacked into the Canal End. The Dubs couldn't rely on the Hill this time. Dublin lead by a slight margin heading into the final stages of the game. Jason knew a goal was needed to put this match to bed. As Whelo brought the ball up from midfield, Jason made a clever run into space. Jason collected the ball, turned his marker and then fired a goal past the keeper.

Jason could hear a roar ripple from Hill 16 just as the ball hit the net. The rest of the stadium exploded soon after. The sound of the roar was so loud it almost lifted Jason off the ground. He turned and saluted everyone on the Hill. They roared back. Jason had never known anything like this in sport. What an adrenaline rush!

Dublin held out to win by six points, 2-12 to 2-06. The whole Dublin team ran to wave at the Hill after the final whistle.

The Dublin senior team would beat Meath to make it a Dublin double. Jason realised that afternoon that being a Dublin footballer was a buzz unlike anything he'd ever known.

CHAPTER 18

LEARNING HOW TO LOSE

T hings were getting serious now for Jason and Dublin. An All-Ireland final was in touching distance. All they had to do was beat Galway in the semifinal. Easier said than done, says you! All week, their coaches had prepared them for a true test.

'Their forwards, these lads like Padráic Joyce and Michael Donnellan, are going to win Galway an All-Ireland someday, mark my words,' Uncle Brian said.

Leaving Cert results were out that week. Jason was relieved. He did just enough to avoid repeating. All across Dublin, students celebrated in discos. It was not the ideal week to prepare for an All-Ireland semifinal! It was great fun going into town with everyone from St Vincent's. Some of the lads were celebrating because they got enough points to go to Trinity or UCD. Some lads like Jason were happy to have done enough to pass the exam. Either way, they'd spent years together in secondary school. Jason was sad to say goodbye to them.

Playing Galway would be a huge test for the Dublin backs. Jason was carrying a knee injury into the match. He scored the first point of the game by fisting over from close range, but the game got away from him. Galway scored a brilliant goal in the first half and built a sizeable lead. On the other end of the field, the Dublin half backs couldn't get anything to stick. Jason's teammates couldn't get him the ball. He was growing extremely frustrated, and the game was getting away from them.

Finally, in the second half, with the lead at six, Whelo decided to shake things.

'Jason,' he shouted. 'Go into centre forward. Drop back into play. Make a difference from there.'

Jason was determined to make up for lost time.

He was picked up by the Galway centre half back.

'Mind yourself, hot shot,' the Galway lad said, and threw Jason a dig into the ribs.

Jason knew nothing would come easy in this position. But if he could win the ball, he could pull Dublin back into it. It was a bit like being back playing point guard for St Vincent's.

The digs, and the verbals, kept coming from the Galway lad. When the Dublin half back skyed a ball in from opposite 65, Jason jumped, caught the ball, and was immediately cleaned out of it by his marker.

It was a clumsy tackle, sure. But Jason reacted as if it was intended to hurt him. He won a free, but he didn't care. He got up and threw the ball right in the face of the Galway centre half back. He snapped.

A few of the Galway backs ran over to him and grabbed his jersey. They all started to jostle. While it felt good in the moment to release his anger, Jason immediately realised that he'd done something you can never do on a GAA pitch. You can never lose your temper, no matter how much your marker winds you up. The referee reversed his call, and opted for a throw ball. The match was gone for Dublin. Jason couldn't wait for the full-time whistle to come so he could be anywhere else.

There was so much disappointment in the dressing room after. Half the team was in tears. The incident with Jason and the Galway centre half back summed up Dublin's day.

'I'm sorry Jason, but you just can't treat opponents like that. No matter what they say or do to you. When you snap, they've won,' Alan said. Jason knew he was right.

'Lads, we'll learn from this. Sport will teach you many lessons. One of them is how to lose,' Brian said.

That night, the incident was singled out on the *Sunday Game* highlights of the match. The pundits were not complimentary.

'This is not how young players should be behaving. This is not how we play Gaelic games,' one pundit, a former intercounty manager, said.

It was a terrible feeling to be talked about on TV like this. Jason was only used to being praised.

The next day, when the pain of defeat started to ease, Jason sat down with his mam and Bill.

'Sport is all about self-control, Jason,' Bill said. 'These lads are looking to get an edge on you. They want you to snap out at them. You need to be the bigger man.'

It reminded Jason of the abuse he'd received back in Ballyhea. Sometimes, he just snapped. Something would provoke him, and his temper would flare.

It was scary how strong his temper was. There was anger inside him which was hard to control sometimes.

'The best sportspeople learn how to take their aggression and turn it into something positive,' Bill said.

Jason knew he was right. It would just take some time to figure out how to change.

CHAPTER 19

BIG TIME CALLING

Barely a few weeks had passed from the semi-final when Jason got another phone call about GAA.

His mam handed him the phone.

'Jay, it's Paul from Na Fianna here. I got a call today from the Dublin County Board. The Dublin seniors have a challenge game at the weekend against Meath. Dr Pat wants you to link up with the squad.'

Dr Pat was the Dublin manager. He was desperately trying to coach Dublin to their first All-Ireland win since 1983.

This was not a call Jason was expecting. Dublin had won their All-Ireland semifinal against Leitrim and now had an All-Ireland final to prepare for against Down in three weeks' time. Jason had hoped to be involved with the Dublin under-21s next season if he was lucky. Never in a million years did he expect to be joining up with the Dublin senior panel three weeks before the All-Ireland! This was all very exciting.

'What was that about?' his mam asked.

'They want me to play for the Dublin seniors in a challenge match at the weekend!' Jason said.

He couldn't believe his luck. Mam and Bill and hugged Jason.

The night before the match he rang Uncle Eddie on the phone.

'Listen, whatever happens, treat this as a future audition for the senior team. Make sure Dr Pat can put a name to your face by the end of it,' he said.

Jason's mate Robbo from the minor team had also gotten a call. They arrived for the team bus that day and Dr Pat pulled them aside.

'Listen lads, we're going to throw you in for twenty minutes towards the end of the game. We're trying to give some of the lads a run out here today, but we need yourselves to finish the match for us.'

The match was on in Nobber in County Meath. Jason sat in the front of the bus. On the journey up, Jason listened to his Gaelic football heroes tell stories. He hung on their every word. He didn't want to put a toe wrong in front of his idols.

Jason got nervous even looking at them. There was Charlie Redmond, Dublin's star forward. He was a fireman and a favourite of Hill 16. There was Mick Galvin and Paul Bealin, who everyone called Bealo, and Paul Clarke, who everyone called Clarkey.

With twenty minutes left in the challenge match, he got the nod from Dr Pat, just as he'd promised. Jason felt like a boy next to these huge men. Senior football was a different kettle of fish altogether. Lads were scrapping and tussling. The refereeing was pretty loose since it was a challenge match.

'Just run the legs off these Meath fellas,' Dr Pat had told him when he subbed him on, and that's what Jason intended to do.

He expended a lot of energy, and didn't make any huge mistakes.

In the changing room after the match, Dr Pat

approached Jason and Robbo.

'That was great, lads. Listen, we could use some young legs around the place as we prepare for the All-Ireland. We could use you at training over the next two weeks if you had the time.'

'For sure,' Jason said.

'Absolutely,' Robbo said.

Jason was stunned. It was like hitting the jackpot on a scratch card.

'You were running so much, it was making *me* tired,' said Paul Bealin to Jason. 'You know what we'll call you from now on? The Little Bullet. That's what you are! The Little Bullet.'

It was an incredible feeling to drive over to Parnell Park on the following Tuesday.

'Let me get this right,' Gar had said to him that weekend. 'You're part of the Dublin senior panel now? We're two weeks from the All-Ireland final and you're in the Dublin panel!'

'Not exactly,' Jason said, slightly embarrassed. 'I won't be part of the match-day squad or anything like that. I'm just training with the lads before the match.'

'Sounds like you're part of the Dublin squad to

me,' Gar said.

Jason admitted it was pretty crazy. Six months ago, Jason had never played Gaelic football as a member of a club. Now he was on the fringes of the Dublin senior team. He'd leapfrogged loads of talented players in the under-21 team. This had all happened very, very quickly!

Jason tried to be as professional as possible at training. Dublin had a huge match to prepare for. They hadn't won an All-Ireland final since 1983, and Jason could tell how badly they wanted to win it. Meath had overtaken them as the kings of Leinster. When Dublin had battled past them, they'd fallen at the final hurdle, like in 1992 when Donegal beat them in the All-Ireland final.

Their final training session was the Thursday before the All-Ireland final. When Jason got back to the dressing room, there was an envelope on top of his kitbag. He opened it up and found a ticket to the All-Ireland final and the post match banquet.

'Deadly,' he said.

'Thanks for help, Jayo,' Dr Pat said. 'The lads have all been impressed with you. We'll be seeing you again, no doubt.'

'Hopefully,' Jason said.

There was huge anticipation for the All-Ireland around Dublin. There was nothing quite like All-Ireland final day in the capital, especially when the Dubs were involved. Blue flags hung all around the city.

'You should be playing for Dublin today, not up in the stands,' Uncle Brian said to Jason that morning over breakfast. 'Dublin need a player like you.'

'Ah here!' Jason said. 'It's the All-Ireland final, and I'm just eighteen!'

'It doesn't matter,' Uncle Eddie said. 'You'd give them something different. Imagine throwing you in at sixty minutes when the defence is starting to tire.'

Jason wasn't sure he was ready for such a big occasion, but he was flattered to even be considered for the match. It was a rain-soaked day, but there was a huge atmosphere on Jones's Road and all around Croke Park ahead of kickoff. Jason got into the match in time to watch the minor All-Ireland final between Kerry and Galway, who'd defeated Dublin in the semifinal. It was a brilliant match. There was some great footballing talent on the rise in Ireland. Jason hoped the day would come when he and his Dublin teammates could prove they were as good.

The Hill was full of Dublin supporters singing 'Molly Malone' and 'Come On You Boys in Blue'. The Down supporters dressed in black and red. They brought plenty of noise.

It was fascinating to watch the match having trained with the team. Jason knew exactly what Dublin's game plan was. Unfortunately, Down had a plan of their own. Their star forward Mickey Linden ran riot. Charlie missed a penalty and Dublin were beaten again, 0-15 to 0-13

Jason was gutted for the lads. He knew firsthand how much work they had put in and how badly they wanted to win the All-Ireland for their supporters. They needed an All-Ireland win to prove they were a great team.

Jason wondered if the result would have been any different if he'd played, even as a sub.

As Jason was leaving Croke Park, a stranger in a Dublin jersey approached Jason. In the past, when strangers approached him, Jason got a bit nervous and would prepare himself for a comment about his appearance.

'I've seen you play for the Dubs, son,' the man said. He had a thick Dublin accent. 'You're exactly the kind of player we need. We need new blood or else we'll keep losing finals like today. Keep your head on straight son and you'll be starting for Dublin next year, mark my words.'

'Fair enough,' Jason said, with a smile. It was just one man's opinion. But deep down Jason found himself agreeing. He knew he could hold his own with the best Gaelic footballers in Ireland. It didn't matter how old he was.

He just needed someone to take a chance on him.

CHAPTER 20

A JUGGLING ACT

It was the autumn of 1994. Jason was eighteen. He thought he was at his last training session for the UCD soccer team at Belfield on the UCD campus. Jason had been training with UCD for the past few weeks. He wouldn't miss the long bus ride across the city centre. But as he walked around the campus, he felt jealous of all the students living the dream at university.

That autumn, Jason realised he might have made a mistake not studying hard enough for the Leaving Cert. Jason had done enough to avoid repeating, but he was beginning to realise there was more to the world than sport. He had been consumed with sport and hadn't thought enough about third-level education. He knew his nan was right: education was the most important thing in life, even more important than sport!

That week, Jason received the phone call he'd been dreaming of.

'Jason, this is the Dublin County Board calling,' a voice said. 'You've been selected for the Dublin senior team for the upcoming League campaign.'

This was incredible news. Jason was still eighteen and he'd been invited to play with the Dublin seniors.

In those days, the League kicked off in the autumn, just weeks after the Championship ended. It was brilliant to be training with the best Gaelic footballers in Dublin.

Jason had some time on his hands. Two of Jason's mates with the Dublin minors, Mick and Eamon, had just started at UCD. They were doing trials for the UCD soccer team during the preseason, and invited Jason along.

'Join us for the trials,' Mick said. 'It's a bit of craic.'

'But I'm not a student at UCD,' Jason said.

'It doesn't matter for the moment,' Mick said.

UCD played in the League of Ireland first division and were a pretty serious side. Jason liked the sound of the challenge.

'Of course, I'll come!' Jason said, without hesitation. Because he was eighteen, he couldn't play with St Kevin's Boys anymore. He was on the lookout for a regular game of football. He'd been training with the UCD lads for more than a month, and he'd loved every second of it. The season started in two weeks, and Jason knew it was time to say goodbye. At the end of the day, only UCD students could play for the UCD team.

As the lads did their stretches to warm, up Larry, the UCD coach, approached Jason.

'It's been great having you down here, Jason,' Larry said. 'It's a pity we'll have to say goodbye to you.'

'Ah yeah, I understand. It's no problem. Thanks for having me in for the kickabout!'

As they were chatting, Dr Tony O'Neill, the head of sport at UCD walked by. Jason had gotten familiar with him during the past few weeks.

'Don't leave without grabbing a word with me after training, son,' Dr Tony said. 'I'd like to chat to you about something.'

'Sure thing,' Jason said.

There were some good footballers involved at these training sessions, but Jason was as good as any of them. The lads played a game of eleven-a-side, and Jason made a nuisance of himself. In a few weeks' time, these lads would be putting themselves up against the best of the League of Ireland First Division. Jason was certain he could play to their standard.

Jason said goodbye to everybody after showering. All the UCD players shook his hand as if he was a teammate. Jason was genuinely sad to be leaving. He felt like one of the team.

'Pity I didn't listen to Nanny and study harder for the Leaving,' he said to himself as he walked over to Dr Tony's office.

'Hiya, Jason,' Dr Tony said, as Jason poked his head into his office.

'Listen Dr Tony,' Jason said. 'I just wanted to say thanks for the opportunity to train with the lads. It's been great craic. Best of luck in the League.'

'I was hoping to chat to you about that, Jason,' Dr Tony said. 'We see how talented you are on the football pitch. We'd like to offer you a scholarship to play soccer and do a diploma course here in health and safety at UCD. Would that interest you?'

'Of course it would!' Jason said.

'This would allow you to study here with us at UCD and play for the soccer team.'

'I'd love that,' Jason said.

'Brilliant. As a player for UCD, you're also entitled to a salary of £240 a month. And you get a bonus of a tenner for every match we win, so there's plenty of incentive to win matches.'

'I'm delighted,' Jason said. 'There's only one issue.'

'What's that?' Dr Tony said.

'If the Dublin GAA invite me to join the senior team for the Championship, GAA will have to be my top priority.'

'We can find a solution that fits everybody,' Dr Tony said.

'Then sign me up!' Jason said.

Jason couldn't believe his luck. He was going to get paid to play sport, plus he now had a course at UCD. Things were coming together.

'Are you worried about how you'll juggle everything? There's a lot on your plate,' Uncle Brian said after Jason told him the news.

'Absolutely not,' Jason said. 'I just want to play.'

'Fair play, Jason. It's important to do what you love in life,' Uncle Brian said. 'But as you get older, a coach will some day ask you to commit fully to one sport.'

'Well, until then,' Jason said. 'I'm just going to lap this up.'

It seemed manageable. The Dublin footballers' league games were mostly played on Sunday afternoons, while UCD played a lot of their games on Thursday nights.

Jason loved the madness of it. He just wanted to play sport, and playing for the Dublin Gaelic football team and the UCD soccer team meant he'd be travelling up and down the country every weekend.

It meant he was in great shape for playing Gaelic football. Dr Pat, the Dublin GAA coach, had pulled him aside at the first training session of the 1995 season.

'We need fresh talent next year if we're ever going to win the All-Ireland,' he said. 'So consider the league an audition. If you're good enough, we'll keep you on. We'll be starting you at corner forward against Kerry in the first match of the league.

Does that sound OK?'

'I can handle it,' Jason said.

The Dublin footballers were all icons to him, but because he'd trained with them just a few months ago, he didn't feel nervous in their company. For the match, the Dublin team got the train to Killarney from Heuston Station. When Jason met his teammates on the train, it suddenly got very real for him. He was a Dublin footballer now.

'Many lads have done well at minor level only to never be heard of again,' Uncle Eddie had told Jason that autumn. Jason knew a few lads who were good once but had lost focus. That made Jason even more determined to seize his opportunity.

The match was on at Fitzgerald Stadium. It was fitting that it was Dublin's great rivals Kerry who were the opposition in Jason's first match with Dublin. Dessie Farrell, Jason's old role model at St Vincent's, was starting at centre forward, and Jason was determined not to let him down. A small contingent of Dublin supporters had made the trip down from Dublin and they made their voices heard. Jason struggled to make a dent in the game. It was a huge step up from minor. Deep into the second half, with Dublin trailing by three, Dessie broke free from his marker and claimed the ball in Kerry's 45. Jason sensed he had suddenly had a bit of daylight on his marker. Dessie spotted his run and played Jason into space with a clever pass.

Now Jason was twenty yards from goal, with just the keeper to beat. He could hear all of the old traditional GAA fans in his own head saying 'pop it over the bar, take your handy score.'

Jason wasn't like one of those old-school GAA people. Dublin needed a goal and Jason rocketed a shot past the Kerry keeper. Goal for Dublin!

It was Jason's first goal as a Dublin senior footballer. He pointed at Dessie as if to say 'thanks for that', but Dessie was already up the field getting ready to help defend the Kerry kickout. In the end Kerry won by a point. Jason left Killarney with a feeling he'd never forget. He'd scored a goal in his first match for the Boys in Blue.

When he looked at his fixture list for December, two dates in December stood out. One Saturday evening, UCD were playing against Finn Harps up in Ballybofey in Donegal, a good four hours from home. The next afternoon, the Dublin footballers were playing Donegal at Croke Park in Dublin.

'We need some ideas here,' Jason said to Dr Tony. 'Otherwise I won't be able to play. That bus won't be back in Dublin in time.'

Dr Tony scratched his chin.

'What if I put you in a taxi after the match?'

'All the way from Donegal to Dublin?'

'If it gets us three points, I'm all for it,' Dr Tony said.

And so as soon as the full-time whistle blew in Ballybofey, Jason grabbed his kitbag and sprinted for the taxi that was parked just outside Finn Park.

'Will you take me to Dublin?' Jason said with a laugh.

'Hop in,' the driver said.

Jason was in bed before 1am. He just tried to sleep and recover so he'd be ready to go the next day.

Jason was named to start at full forward for the Dubs the next day. Jason felt pretty fresh, all things considered. It was a tight match. Dublin attacked into Hill 16 in the first half. Jason spotted the Donegal keeper slowly dawdling with the ball at his feet so he raced up, stole the ball and put it past him. It was the cheekiest goal he'd ever scored on a GAA pitch.

Jason loved scoring it right in front of the Hill. He waved his hands up and down to celebrate, and tried to egg the supporters on.

One of his teammates, Sean, raced over and grabbed him by the collar.

'This isn't the Premiership, Jason, that's not how we celebrate goals in the GAA.'

'Fair enough,' Jason shouted, with a sly smile.

He felt like the bold kid in class. As the game went on, Jason asked himself what had he really done that was so bad. He'd scored a big goal and enjoyed a moment with the Dublin supporters. He'd expressed himself. The GAA could use more people like him who weren't afraid to show that they enjoyed playing the game. The GAA was stuck very much in its traditions, he thought.

Jason finished the match with 1-1 to his name. He got home that night and stretched himself out on the couch.

'Will we order a pizza? I think you've earned it,' his mam said, with a big smile.

'Thanks Mam,' Jason said. 'I'm starving!'

CHAPTER 21

ONE OF THE BOYS IN GREEN

There was only one thing threatening to slow down Jason's progress with the Dublin football team, and that was Jason's success on the soccer field.

Jason had been flying with UCD. Now every time he picked up a newspaper, there was a story about him signing with a Premiership club.

'It's Newcastle this week,' Uncle Brian said and handed him a copy of the *Evening Herald*.

'Newcastle plot bid for UCD starlet,' the headline read.

'News to me,' Jason said with a laugh. It was great to be mentioned for these transfers, but neither he nor anyone in his family had had any contact from these clubs.

'It's a good problem to have, I suppose,' Uncle Brian said.

He had done so well he was called into the Ireland under-21 squad for their match with England that March. Training with the Ireland under 21s would only help his chances of getting a professional contract.

The Ireland under 21s played England in Dalymount Park in Dublin.

Dalymount had witnessed many famous Irish football nights. Ireland had beaten the USSR here 3-0 in 1974. Jason and his uncles had seen Ireland play Italy here in 1985. Now it was Jason's turn. He was wearing the green jersey of Ireland. Best of all, Dalymount was just a few kilometres from his house, in Phibsboro. This part of Dublin was just overflowing with Irish sporting history.

Jason and his UCD teammate Mick were both named to the subs bench. Their manager Seamus had told them they likely wouldn't feature since they were so new to the squad.

'Just soak it all in, lads. In a year's time, we'll be turning to you.'

Training had been brilliant. There was a very talented generation of Irish footballers coming up. The starting goalkeeper was a sound lad from Lifford in Donegal named Shay Given. Shay was on the books at Blackburn Rovers, who were leading contenders for the Premier League that season. There was another lad named Stephen Carr who'd played underage with the Stella Maris club in Dublin. Tottenham Hotspur had signed him, and he'd made his Premier League debut before turning twenty-one.

Training with these lads made Jason think he could play in England someday.

'Do you see the Sky Sports camera there?' Mick said.

'Crazy to think this is going to be broadcast all across Ireland and the UK,' Jason said.

'All the Premiership scouts will be watching,' Mick said. His eyes lit up. The thought of it was enough to make you dizzy, but Jason was getting used to the attention.

'This is a serious English side,' Seamus had said before kickoff. 'There's lads like Gary Neville and Nicky Butt who'll definitely represent England at senior level. We'll have to dig deep to beat them.'

It was such a surreal experience. To stand for the

anthems and hear 'God Save The Queen' and then 'Amhrán na bhFiann' gave him goose bumps. It was a hard-fought game, but England scored two second-half goals and won 2-0.

Even though he hadn't played, Jason felt gutted after the match. It never felt good to lose to England. But his bad mood did not last long.

Before Jason and Mick could leave the dressing room, they were approached by a man wearing an FAI blazer.

'Lads, thanks for a great week of training. I have an opportunity that might be of interest.'

'Go on,' Jason said.

'To promote the League of Ireland, we're giving two League of Ireland players the opportunity to train with the senior team for a week. You lads did brilliantly all week for the under 21s and I was wondering what you'd think of joining up with the senior team next week, before the match with Northern Ireland.'

'Absolutely!' Mick said.

'What does it involve?' Jason asked.

'Basically you'll stay in the team hotel all week. You'll go to training sessions. You'll travel with the lads. You'll be treated like a senior Ireland international for the week.'

Mick and Jason looked at each other like they'd just won the lottery.

And so a week later, he was dropped at a hotel out by Dublin airport. He and Mick walked into the lobby and saw all of the great Irish players of the day hanging out. Jason was starstruck. There was Roy Keane of Manchester United, Niall Quinn of Manchester City, Paul McGrath of Aston Villa and Jason McAteer of Liverpool. Phil Babb of Liverpool approached them. Jason watched him every week on television.

'Best of luck this week, lads. I'm Phil Babb and let me know if you need anything,' he said.

'Thanks a million, Phil,' Jason said.

And then a big bald man with a loud Geordie accent walked into the hotel and started shaking the hands of the players. Eventually he worked his way over to Jason.

'Jason, let me introduce you to Big Jack,' Phil said.

'Pleasure to meet you, sir,' Jason said.

'Jack, just call me Jack,' he said, and stuck out his hand. Jack was Irish royalty, having managed Ireland to the World Cup in 1990 and 1994. It was like meeting a proper celebrity. People queued up to have a word with him.

The kitman handed Jason his training kit for the week. Jason and Micko sat side-by-side at dinner. Jason had to pinch himself a few times that week. It was crazy to be surrounded by all of these famous footballers.

They trained in the morning in Malahide. They played a game of As vs Bs and Jason found himself on a team going against the likes of Roy Keane. He couldn't believe it.

Jason also got an insight into what life as a professional footballer was really like. After their morning training session, there was a lot of down time in the hotel! A lot of the players played cards in the hotel lobby. They weren't like the millionaire footballers you'd read about in the English newspapers. They were fun lads who loved football, but loved a laugh just as much.

But as the week went on, the mood in camp got more serious. The match was in Dublin and all the talk in camp was about getting three points.

Jason travelled with the team to Lansdowne Road

for the match. 32,200 people were in attendance: a full house. The atmosphere in the grounds was brilliant. Niall Quinn scored early in the second half for Ireland from a free kick, and Jason heard the famous Lansdowne Roar, when all the fans shouted in unison. Northern Ireland equalised in the seventy-thirdrd minute and escaped with a draw.

'Two points dropped,' Roy said in the dressing room after the match. He looked angry. The disappointment was obvious. Even if Ireland hadn't got the win, Jason had learned so much in the past few weeks.

He arrived back at his mam's house that evening.

'Well if it isn't yourself?' his mam said. 'Long time, no see.'

Jason had been away from home for just over a week, but it was like he'd been abroad for a holiday. After a week in the presence of Roy Keane and Jack Charlton, it was good to be home and be just another nineteen-year-old.

'How're you fixed for some steak and chips?' his mam said. 'This isn't a hotel though. We don't do room service.'

Jason laughed, 'Home sweet home!'

CHAPTER 22

LIVERPOOL COME KNOCKING

Jason was training with UCD at the Belfield Bowl during the final weeks of the soccer season. There was no time to be tired or over-whelmed for Jason. Everything was happening. The season had gone brilliantly with UCD. At just nine-teen, he'd be named PFAI Player of the Year for the first division. It was an amazing honour.

Towards the end of training, Dr Tony came sprinting over to them.

'Lads, you're never going to believe this,' he said. 'I've convinced a big football club to come over and play us in a friendly.'

The club had turned one hundred years old last season, and there'd been a lot of speculation that there'd be a big match to commemorate the occasion.

'Who is it?' Jason said.

'Liverpool Football Club!'

'What?' Mick said.

'You're having a laugh,' Jason said.

'I'm just off the phone with Anfield,' he said. 'No joke, they're coming over to play us a few days after the Premier League season ends. I've booked Lansdowne Road. I think we'll sell it out.'

Jason thought this was all a cod, but Dr Tony wasn't laughing. Jason and his teammates couldn't believe it. He was a Liverpool supporter, so it would be a dream come true to play against them.

He rang Uncle Eddie after training.

'Don't treat it like a friendly, treat it like a trial,' Uncle Eddie said. 'You'll never get a better chance to make an impression on them.' Being a Liverpool player was Jason's ultimate sporting dream.

The match was held two days after the 1994-95 Premiership season ended. Over 20,000 people bought tickets for the match at Lansdowne Road.

'Don't be intimidated by the kit or the crest on the shirt,' Mick said. 'It's just eleven men against eleven men.'

But when Jason and his UCD teammates filed out of the dressing room and into the tunnel under the stadium and lined up against the Liverpool players, Jason nearly lost it. Inches away from him were many of his Liverpool heroes: Robbie Fowler, Steve McManaman and Jamie Redknapp.

'Good to see you, kid,' said Ireland international Phil Babb to Jason. 'Best of luck out there.'

'You too, Phil,' Jason said. He was surprised that Phil had remembered him.

The atmosphere was unlike any game he'd ever played in. They might as well have been at Anfield. The supporters serenaded their team with 'You'll Never Walk Alone' and 'Fields Of Anfield Road'. Jason was picked to play up front. He could tell straight away that the Liverpool players were leggy after a really long season. They were looking for an easy ninety-minute match before heading off on summer holidays. Jason was determined to run the legs off of them.

Jason also wanted to prove to the Liverpool coaching staff that he was savvy enough to play with the best of the best.

Any time a pass was played in towards him, Jason would anticipate contact from defenders and win a free.

After winning a few frees, the Liverpool back started getting angry and shouting at the referee.

'Ah ref,' the Liverpool defenders shouted. 'You're giving him everything.'

Phil walked up to Jason soon after.

'Be careful mate, or you might get a pair of studs in your ankles!'

'I haven't done anything wrong!' Jason protested, with a smile on his face.

A moment later, another pass came Jason's way. He cleverly let the ball slip between his legs. Phil wasn't ready for it, and the ball passed through Phil's legs as well. Jason tore up the pitch knowing he'd just nut-megged an Ireland international! He could hear the crowd say 'oooooh' as he sprinted up the pitch. He loved entertaining the fans with a flourish of skill.

The match finished 3-1 to Liverpool. Jason didn't get on the score sheet, but he'd created a lot of chances and had a huge impact.

'They weren't that much better than us,' Jason said to Mick in the dressing room.

'Goes to show you,' Mick said. 'They finished fourth in the Premiership. We were first in the League of Ireland first division.'

Jason left Lansdowne Road feeling like he was on cloud nine. He really felt like he belonged amongst the best players in Ireland and England. Afterwards, they all attended a reception for both teams at a fancy hotel.

In the hotel lobby, while he was chatting to his teammates, Jason noticed the Liverpool manager Roy Evans walking straight towards him.

'Jason, you were tremendous out there this evening,' the Liverpool manager said. 'We'd like you to join us over at Liverpool for a bit of training for a few days. We'll see what happens from there. Would you be up for that?'

Jason was stunned.

'It'd be a dream come true,' Jason said.

'Brilliant,' Roy said and moved on. 'We'll be in touch.'

Jason couldn't believe his own good fortune. The only problem was he didn't know when he'd get the time to get to Liverpool. He was in the Ireland under 21 squad for a Euro qualifier against Austria the next month, and then there was the small business of the Leinster championship with the Dublin Gaelic football team.

Jason made a point of buying all of the newspapers the next morning. His photos were all over the back pages. Not only were they praising his performance against Liverpool, they were reporting that English clubs like Everton were now seriously interested in signing him. Young Irish players were receiving as much as £1 million a year to play in the Premiership. Jason felt like his whole life was about to change.

'It's all happening for you, Jason,' his mam said.

'I just want to be sure I take my chance,' he said.

'Just be sure that whatever you do, you're happy doing it,' Bill said.

Jason was called into the Ireland under 21 squad for their match against Austria that June. Jason was determined to win his first cap with the Ireland under 21 team this time around.

He treated every training session like his entire footballing career depended on it. Some of his teammates – lads who were already playing with Premiership clubs – already had a place in the team and didn't have to try as hard. Jason would have to fight for everything he got.

'If I anger a few people on the way, oh well,' Jason said to Uncle Brian

He could tell his teammates didn't appreciate his intensity. But Jason could also tell his manager respected him for it. For the Austria match, he was named to start on the bench, but his manager Maurice gave him the signal in the second half.

'Jason, you've earned this, go out there and enjoy yourself,' Maurice said, as Jason waited to run onto the field.

Jason wasn't long in setting up a goal. When the referee blew the game up, Ireland had defeated Austria 3-0 and Jason had never felt prouder.

'I've represented Ireland in basketball and football now,' he said. 'Remember those kids who told me to go back to my own country when I was small? I've played for Ireland in two sports.'

'You didn't let them stop Jason, you rose above them,' his mam said. 'How are you going to celebrate?'

'By relaxing!' he said. 'I've got my first Dublin championship game in two weeks!'

CHAPTER 23

CHAMPO

It was June 1995. Jason was nineteen. It was the day of Dublin's first game of the 1995 Leinster Championship. The Dubs were playing Louth. It was a game the Dubs should win, but no one was taking the opponents lightly. This was knockout football: lose and go home.

In the last training sessions before the Louth game, Jason could tell how serious his teammates were about winning the All-Ireland. He could also tell all of the big defeats had taken a toll on their confidence.

On the Thursday before training, Dr Pat addressed the panel.

'Look lads, we all know the situation, but I'll put

it out there in black and white for you,' Dr Pat said. 'The window is closing on us. This has to be our year.'

The Dublin players didn't need to be reminded of it. In 1991, they'd lost an epic series to Meath. Dublin had lost the 1992 All-Ireland final to Donegal. Derry beat them in the All-Ireland semifinal in 1993. Then Down had beat them in the 1994 All-Ireland final.

'This is my last chance, lads,' Dr Pat said. 'If we don't win the Sam Maguire, I'll be gone. A lot of you lads will too. For all the work we've done, we owe it to ourselves to win an All-Ireland.'

'And luckily we've got lads like Jason to push us all on,' Dessie said.

'Exactly,' Dr Pat said.

'Now, I'll give you the fifteen to start against Louth,' Dr Pat said. Jason was confident he'd be named in the starting team, but didn't want to jump to any conclusions.

Dr Pat read out the full fifteen and Jason wasn't on the list.

He wasn't disappointed. He was determined.

'I'll just have to prove to them that I belong,'

Jason said.

The match took place in Navan. Louth had no track record of beating Dublin, but there was no room for being complacent. This was knockout football.

'We lose this and our summer's over before we even get started,' Dr Pat said.

Jason knew he was going to get a run at some stage of the match that afternoon. He couldn't really explain how he knew. He just knew he'd make his Dublin championship debut today. He just tried to focus on the game that was about to take place, but his brain was full of excitement and worry.

'Alright lads,' Charlie said, as the bus pulled into Páirc Tailteann. 'Today we take our first step towards Sam Maguire.'

The car park at Páirc Tailteann was thronged with Dublin supporters. They were waiting to welcome the Dublin team to Navan. As Dr Pat led the team off the bus, the Dubs fans parted and gave them room to walk into the dressing room.

Jason grabbed his kit bag from the bottom of the bus, as Dublin fans around him sang and cheered. He felt a burst of pride to have been selected to wear this shirt. This was different from playing soccer with UCD. He couldn't explain how it was different, but it was. He thought of being a boy and watching his Dublin heroes win the Sam Maguire. But Jason also felt a responsibility to the jersey, and a pressure too. He couldn't let these people down.

When Jason arrived in the dressing room, he took his jersey and shorts from his kitbag. He realised right away that there was a problem. He was too short to reach the hooks to hang up his tracksuit! They clearly had designed these dressing rooms for bigger men! He considered his options. He could stand up on the bench. But no, he couldn't do that. The whole team would be rolling around laughing. He couldn't leave his tracksuit on the bench either. What would he do?

'Do you want a hand there, young fella?' Clarkey said, with a sly smile.

'Ah thanks Clarkey, I'd be lost without you,' Jason said, and handed him his track suit.

He'd been given the jersey number 21. He put the jersey on, and he realised it was about four sizes too big for him! Most lads playing Championship football were much bigger than he was. Jason had his trusty black Reebok boots on. He wasn't too worried about the size of his jersey, just as long as his boots didn't let him down.

But once the warm-ups began, Jason realised pretty quickly that he looked more like a mascot than a senior intercounty footballer. His tracksuit was massive. His jersey underneath was huge. Meanwhile his teammates looked like giants. Jason tried not to think too much about it!

It was an overcast afternoon. Jason took his place on the subs bench. From the second the ball was thrown in, Jason could tell this match was being played at a level of intensity he had never seen before. The tackles went flying in. A few sly digs were thrown. No one wanted to give an inch.

Louth were intent on making things very hard for Dublin, but the Dubs controlled the scoreboard early. Then after twenty minutes, Sean, one of the Dublin forwards, went down with an injury. The physios sprinted over to him.

'Looks serious,' Jason said.

That second, Dr Pat turned around and looked Jason right in the eye.

'Jason, you're on.'

Jason didn't even think. He ripped off his huge tracksuit and sprinted onto the pitch. One of the selectors handed him a white piece of paper, with his name on it, saying he was coming on for Sean. He ran straight to the referee with it.

It was the longest run of his life. He was terrified he might drop the paper or tear it and the referee might not let him on the pitch.

'Here you go, sir,' he said, when he finally reached the referee.

'C'mon Jay,' Charlie said. 'Show them your pace.'

Jason nodded. Now that he was on the pitch, Jason could see just how small he was compared to everyone else on the pitch. It felt like men against boy.

'Don't be afraid,' Jason told himself. 'They can't hurt what they can't stop.'

Jason knew he had an immediate advantage because he was a brand-new commodity. The Louth defenders wouldn't be prepared for him. They had no idea how fast he was. And so just seconds after coming onto the pitch, he tore up the wing, right into space. A pass came into him, then he played a 1-2 with a teammate. Just as Jason stepped into the penalty box, one of the Louth players tackled him to the ground. As he fell, another Louth defender tripped him and accidentally kneed Jason in the head.

Jason was half dazed when he realised the referee had signalled for a penalty. Charlie ran over to him and tried to lift him from the ground.

'Fair play, Jason,' he said. 'You won a penalty with your first possession!'

'Thanks,' Jason said. He was still a bit groggy from the tackle.

'But listen to me,' Charlie said, pulling Jason aside. 'Don't ever allow them the chance to see you're in pain. That means they're winning. You just have to dust yourself off and get right up.'

'Okay, sure thing,' Jason said. It was easy for Charlie to say – Charlie was a big man. Jason was about nine stone!

Clarkey stood over the penalty. He missed! It was a massive let downfor Dublin, but Jason felt confident in his own ability to scare these Louth boys.

All of a sudden, Jason became the focal point of the Dublin attack. He collected the ball between the 21 and the 45 and darted past his marker. The

Louth defense was at sixes and sevens trying to contain him. Eventually the Louth defence decided they couldn't stop him, and so they just decided to wrestle him to the ground.

The Dublin supporters tried to lend Jason a hand. Any time a Louth defender tried to tackle him off the ball, they'd shout and call for the referee to take action.

'Next time they try tackling you like that,' Charlie said. 'Just sprint over to the umpire and let them know you're being fouled. Then we'll see what they do.'

Jason did just that when the next rough tackle came in. He stepped out of it and ran towards the umpires as the play went on around them.

'They're wrestling me to the ground,' Jason shouted. 'They're not letting me play.'

The umpires didn't know what to do. Neither did the Louth defense. Safe to say they'd never seen a player like Jason Sherlock before.

The ball came back to the Dublin end just before full time. Jason had the ball close to goal and took his man on. He soloed past him and left the Louthman in his wake. But then another huge tackle came in from his blind side, and Jason felt a shoulder bang right into his head.

Jason was on the pitch again.

The referee blew for a foul and gave the tackler a yellow card.

Jason dusted himself off. But as he did, he could hear Charlie calling him over.

'Jay,' he shouted. 'Get over here. You won the free. You're taking it.'

Jason was shocked. Charlie had been Dublin's free-taker for years. Now he was handing the ball off. Jason had never taken a free in his life.

'I can't take frees, that's not my job,' Jason said.

'You're taking it,' Charlie said, handing the ball off. 'And you're making it.'

Jason stood with the ball, about twenty metres from goal. He felt the eyes of the whole stadium were on him. He knew why Charlie had given him the ball. If he converted, he'd be putting all those Louth defenders in their place. But Jason knew if he missed, he'd be giving the Louth players all of the momentum back. And if he missed a free this close to goal, he knew his teammates and his coaches would doubt if he was fully ready for senior football.

'No pressure then,' Jason said to himself. He took a deep breath and dropped the ball from his hands, and kicked through it with his laces.

The referee raised the white flag and the Dublin supporters roared.

Dublin won by eight points. A strange thing happened at the full-time whistle. About twenty or thirty kids invaded the pitch and ran right for Jason.

'Would you sign my shirt, Jason?' one kid said.

'Can I have your autograph, Jason?' said another.

Jason stayed on the pitch and signed every autograph he could.

Was this what it was like to be famous? he wondered to himself.

CHAPTER 24

DIVIDED LOYALTIES

Jason woke up the next day battered and bruised. Luckily, he had three weeks to recover from the Louth victory. Dublin were playing Laois in the Leinster semifinal.

He felt the aches and pain for a few days after the Louth win. Victory tasted sweet though, sweet enough to make him forget about the pain. It wasn't much different from playing soccer or even basketball. Jason knew he'd always come up against bigger defenders. You didn't get to become a defender if you weren't big and tough. Jason knew he'd just have to be extra committed.

'You don't feel the knocks when you're flying at full speed,' he told his mam after the game.

After the Louth win, Jason received phone calls from friends and family from all over the country. They were all proud of him. Jason couldn't stop thinking about all of his mates down in Ballyhea. He could have ended up a Cork hurler if things had gone in a different direction. Now he was a Dublin footballer.

He showed his number 21 jersey to his Uncle Eddie.

'I'm going to get this jersey framed and send it to Ballyhea.'

'Are you sure about that?' Uncle Eddie said. 'You'll only make one Championship debut for Dublin. You might want to hold onto this shirt.'

'No, no,' Jason said. 'Those guys taught me how to be a GAA player. I want them to have it. I want to say thanks.'

A week later, Jason posted the jersey down to the club

Thanks for showing me the love of GAA, and for sticking with me,' Jason wrote.

Laois were the opposition in the Leinster semifinal. They were a very good team. Jason learned he'd be starting on the Thursday before the game. This one meant a lot to him. Nanny came from Laois, and Jason knew all of his family down there would be watching.

'I'll have divided loyalties on Sunday, Jason,' she said, with a twinkle in her eye. 'But you know I'll also be shouting for you.'

'Thanks, Nanny!'

The match was on in Navan. Dublin fans travelled by their thousands to support their county. Jason was starting at right corner forward, wearing the 15 jersey.

Jason realised pretty quickly that Laois had done their homework. He wasn't having any luck finding space to get on the ball.

'Just be patient, Jason,' Charlie said. 'Your chance will come.'

In the twenty-first minute, Jason collected a pass from Mick Galvin and made a beeline for goal. Jason took the shot off the side of his boot and beat the keeper, only to see the ball bounce off the butt of the goalpost and back into play.

So close! he thought.

Dublin held a small lead heading into the second half. Jason was trying his best to be patient, but he couldn't get his hand on the ball. None of the passes from the half forward line would stick.

With about fifteen minutes left in the game, Jason saw Jim Gavin, one of the Dublin forwards, getting ready to come on.

I'm done, he thought. *That's my game over.*

Instead Jim came on for Mick.

Right as he came on, Jim nodded to Jason as if to say, *Be ready for the pass*.

Moments later, Jim got his hands on the ball and played the pass that Jason had been waiting for all day. Jason caught it and burned past his marker. In the process of beating the Laois full back, Jason felt his right Reebok boot come flying off! That was his shooting boot! There was no time to worry about that, though! Jason knew he might not get a better chance to score a goal today.

He soloed and then tried to hit the ball as hard as he humanly could with his shoe-less foot. It felt strange kicking with his sock, but the ball blasted past the Laois keeper and into the back of the net.

To celebrate, Jason dropped to his knees and pointed his hands towards the sky. It was a real Roy of the Rovers moment – scoring his first Championship goal with just a sock!

Charlie came running over to him. Jason thought he was coming over to praise him for the goal.

'Get up, we have a match to win!' Charlie said. 'And don't forget your boot!'

'Sorry, sorry!' Jason said.

He got his boot on as quickly as he could. Dublin had the breathing room they needed! Late in the game, Dublin won a free. Jason picked up the ball. He stood with his body pointing at Jim. Everyone expected the pass to go to Jim, but Jason knew his teammate Vinnie Murphy was all alone, unmarked in open space. Jason played a no-look pass right to Vinnie. The Laois defense was bamboozled. No one saw it coming. It was a trick Jason had picked up on the basketball court.

'Amazing pass!' Jim shouted.

'You can take the boy out of the basketball court, but you can't take the basketball out of the boy!' Jason replied.

At full time, Jason was swarmed again by autograph seekers. This time, there were at least one hundred kids chasing his autograph.

'I've never seen anything like this before,' Clarkey

said on the bus back to Dublin. 'You're like a pop star to these kids!'

Dublin always had great footballers. Now Jason gave them something they hadn't had in ages: a goal-scoring threat. They'd have to beat their old rivals Meath in the Leinster final. But Jason could tell something was changing in Dublin's mentality. All of a sudden, they were starting to believe they could win the All-Ireland.

When he got home that evening, his nan was waiting for him at the front door.

'I hate seeing my own county lose,' she said. 'But I love seeing my grandson scoring goals for Dublin. Give me a hug.'

Jason started to blush. He loved doing his family proud.

CHAPTER 25

SEAL IT WITH A KISS

It was the last Sunday in July, 1995. It was the day of the Leinster final. Dublin against Meath. Jason was about to get an up-close-and-personal introduction to one of the GAA's greatest rivalries.

In the build-up to the game, Jason had been flooded with interview requests. The phone was ringing off the hook with people looking for him.

'This is getting crazy,' Jason's mam said.

'Tell me about it, Mam! I've only played two Championship games for Dublin!'

Seemingly overnight, Jason had become a national star. And the GAA had never really had a star like Jason before. It helped that he was young. It helped that he played as a forward, creating and scoring goals. And it helped that he looked different from everyone else.

To the Dublin supporters, he was known solely by the nickname Jayo.

'We can't let this hysteria get in the way of your preparation for the Meath game,' Uncle Brian said.

The Dublin management team were also worried that 'Jasonmania' might become a circus, and so they came up with an idea. They were going to help Jason get an agent. That way, Jason wouldn't have to deal with all of these phone calls himself.

'Jason, I'm Kevin Moran, I think I can assist you,' said a man on the phone one night.

Kevin was the perfect candidate. He was a former Dublin footballer. He also had played soccer in England with Manchester United. Now he was an agent for soccer players in the UK. He could help Jason get a trial with Premiership clubs if he was interested.

Of course, Jason had met Kevin a long time ago.

'You probably don't remember this,' Jason said. 'But I met you once years ago, when I was kid. It was after Dublin had won the 1983 All-Ireland, at the reception.'

'I met a lot of people that night!' Kevin said.

They both laughed.

'Look Jason, you're the talk of the whole country,' Kevin said. 'But you don't need all of these distractions.'

'I know. It's hard to focus on training with all of the pandemonium.'

'And I know things are going amazingly, but you also need to think about the next step in your career. I know there's a lot of Premiership clubs interested in signing you.'

'I know,' Jason said. 'But all I care about for the moment is winning Leinster with Dublin, and after that the All-Ireland.'

'That's good to hear,' Kevin said.

Jason felt a lot better knowing that there was someone looking out for his career and his best interests, so he could focus only on sport. Jason agreed to let Kevin become his agent.

There was commotion around Dublin in the days before the match. The media loved Dublin-Meath games.

'We owe these lads one,' Charlie said to the Dublin squad during their final training session before the game.

It was a huge occasion. 64,000 people crammed into Croke Park. It was Jason's first Championship match at Croke Park. He was starting at corner forward again. His spine tingled when he ran out onto the pitch and heard the roar of Hill 16.

As soon as Jason took his place at corner forward right in front of Hill 16, he saw Meath's fiery fullback Colm Coyle running over to mark him. This was no surprise to Jason – Colm was one of the best defenders in Ireland – but when he stood side by side with the Meathman, he knew he was in for seventy minutes of real battle. Jason tried to stand shoulder to shoulder with him, but it was more like his head to Colm's shoulder.

'Best of luck,' Jason said.

Colm didn't reply.

Fair enough, Jason thought.

Over the next seventy minutes, Colm did everything he could to stop Jason. Some of it was legal. A lot of it was illegal. The Dublin fans on the Hill shouted every time Colm got a hold of Jason's jersey or pulled him down. Any time Jason thought he was fouled, he'd sprint over in the direction of the umpires. He was hoping to get in the heads of his marker. But Colm was old-school, and it didn't seem to faze him.

In every other aspect of the game, Dublin were dominating. Dessie was flying it. He kicked an amazing point from the sideline that brought all the Dublin fans to their feet. Charlie kept the scoreboard ticking over.

In the second half, Jason got the ball within scoring distance. He decided to have a go at kicking a point. He tried to get some extra welly on it, but he ended up skying it straight up in the air. It was like a Garryowen in a rugby match. Everyone froze under the ball, but Clarkey had an angle on it, and as the ball came down, he met it with a flying fist and punched it into the back of the goal for Dublin!

'I hope they give me an assist for that one,' Jason shouted as he celebrated with his teammates. There was no way back for Meath now. With a few minutes left in the game, Jason won a free-in near goal after a foul from Colm. Jason was delighted with himself.

As soon as the referee raised his hand and whistled for the free, Jason picked himself up and gave the ref a kiss on the cheek! It was cheeky all right, but Jason couldn't contain himself. He was so delighted to win Leinster. He might not have been in rampaging form, but he'd been a thorn in the side of the Meath defence. And that was enough.

The Hill emptied onto the field at full-time – a full-on Croke Park pitch invasion and now it felt like thousands of people were surrounding him. Some were looking for autographs. Others just wanted to pat him on the back and lift him off the ground and wish him well.

Jason's face was all over the covers of the Irish newspapers the next day.

'Sherlock home and dry' it said on page one of the *Irish Independent*.

He didn't care about any of that though. With a Leinster medal already in his back pocket, why not dream of lifting the Sam Maguire?

CHAPTER 26

BOOM!

All that stood between Dublin and the All-Ireland final now were the Rebels of Cork.

That summer of 1995 was a summer to remember. The weather had been absolutely scorching. Irish people hadn't seen weather like that in decades. It was like being in Spain or Portugal. And maybe the good weather had helped create the conditions that helped Jason thrive.

In the three weeks between the Leinster final and the All-Ireland semifinal, all of Ireland had gone crazy for Jason. There was even a song about him. There was an American rap group called the Out-here Brothers. They had a song that went 'Boom, boom, boom, let me hear you say way-oh, way-oh!'

But the Dublin fans had recorded their own version. It went 'Boom, boom, boom, let me hear you say – Jayo, Jayo!'

All around the city centre, Jason would hear that song. He spent that summer helping at GAA training camps across Dublin. He'd been told there were hundreds of kids across the capital who'd taken on the game that summer just because of him.

'It's amazing isn't it?' Jason said.

'You've only been playing the game for a year!' his mam said.

Jason had spent his childhood worried about seeming different from everyone else. Now, almost overnight, he'd become a hero for young kids across the country. It was crazy. And it had all happened in the blink of an eye.

Cork were one of the best teams in the country, and the hype before the All-Ireland semifinal was huge.

As Jason strode out onto the pitch, the Dublin fans on Hill 16 waved blue flags. There were flags with his name on them 'Sherlock says: it's elementary' one said. 'Jason loves Sam Maguire' another said. He had a little chuckle, but then moved onto the game.

It was clear from the throw-in that Cork were up for this. They'd love nothing more than coming up to the capital and ending Dublin's dream summer.

Jason started at full forward and was marked by Mark O'Connor of Cork. Jason couldn't get a bit of daylight. Mark wouldn't give an inch. Dublin started slow and for the first time that summer, Jason began to worry about their chances.

Dublin only had two points after twenty minutes and trailed by three.

'C'mon Jayo, give us something,' Dr Pat shouted. 'Give us a spark.'

After Dublin claimed a Cork kickout, Jason sensed his moment. The ball was played into space on the right hand side of the pitch. Jason ran into space and claimed the ball. He gave Mark a little shimmy and surged past him. Mark tripped! Jason was one-on-one now with the Cork goalie.

The goalie thought Jason would shoot at the near post, but Jason coolly slotted the ball in on the far post. Croker erupted. It was a class finish. Dublin had the goal it had desperately needed.

'Jason, the darling of Dublin, has lifted the siege!'

exclaimed Marty Morrissey on RTÉ.

Jason could do nothing but shrug his shoulders, as if to say, *Is this really happening?* The momentum of the match was in Dublin's favour now. And it wouldn't swing back.

In the end Jason's goal was the difference between the teams, as Dublin won.

At the full-time whistle, Jason swapped jerseys with Mark.

'Good match,' Mark said.

'Well played,' Jason said.

If Mark hadn't slipped, Jason doubted he would have got the space he needed to score that goal. Sport was all about small margins.

Jason ran over to Hill 16 and raised his fists to the supporters. He was swarmed by Dublin fans.

'Jasonmania has absolutely broken out here at Croke Park,' RTÉ's Michael Lyster said on the TV. 'He's been engulfed by the Dublin supporters.'

Jason was mobbed and in the end, a security person tried to guide him off the pitch. But the supporters didn't care. They grabbed Jason and lifted him onto their shoulders, like he was a general who'd lead his country to victory in war. All the supporters around him jumped and sang 'Boom, boom, boom, let me hear you say Jayo…Jayo!'

All Jason could do was shake his head and laugh. This was the greatest feeling in the world. The Dublin supporters carried their hero around the Croke Park pitch. Dublin were now seventy minutes away from winning the Sam Maguire and they had Jason to thank for getting them this far.

CHAPTER 27

THE GREATEST FEELING

The reward for Dublin's victory against Cork was an All-Ireland final against Tyrone. Even though Tyrone had never won an All-Ireland, a lot of Dublin supporters were worried about their All-Ireland final opposition. The Ulster teams had a history of beating Dublin. Derry, Down and Donegal had all beaten Dublin in recent years in big matches. Ulster football was different, and the northern teams seemed to love getting one up on the Dubs.

But none of those Ulster teams had ever come up against Jason Sherlock.

The pressure was on Jason to deliver. He did everything he could to keep his mind off the pressure of the game. On the day of the final, he decided he'd go to mass. It was a chance to clear his head before the game, and also get a few prayers in for himself and his teammates.

'We've been waiting a long time for an All-Ireland in Dublin, don't forget about us today,' he prayed.

Jason knew this All-Ireland wouldn't be won with prayers. It would be won with guts and heart and hunger. Tyrone would bring plenty of passion to the game as well, so Jason knew he'd have to find a level he'd never reached in his career in order to help his county win the trophy they craved so badly.

Many people wondered how a nineteen-year-old could handle all of this pressure so easily. Jason had put so much pressure on himself as a young basketball player that this didn't really faze him.

Before they got to the All-Ireland final, Dublin had to overcome another hurdle: Jason's fame was getting in the way of their preparations. The 'Jayo' song was all over the radio. You could buy Jayo T-shirts on O'Connell Street. You couldn't pick up a newspaper without an article about him. He was one of the most famous people in Ireland.

This is nuts, Jason thought.

Dublin held a media night the Tuesday before the All-Ireland final at Parnell Park in Dublin. The media would be allowed to turn up to film some interviews at training. The public could come as well. When Jason arrived at the ground, he couldn't believe what he saw. Hundreds and hundreds of people were there just to see him.

'Jayo! Jayo! Jayo!' they all shouted.

He realised quickly that the rest of his teammates weren't going to be able to train with all of these people around. He felt bad. This was a vital training session and he couldn't even get kitted out because of all the supporters.

It took him an hour to sign every autograph.

'It's hard being famous, eh Jay?' said Dessie.

It was crazy. Jason had spent his childhood worshipping Dessie, but all of a sudden, Jason was practically the most famous person in the GAA!

'Look lads, I'm sorry if this is getting in the way of training.'

'It's okay, Jason,' Dr Pat said.

'If anything it's a good thing for us,' Charlie said. 'Usually we'd be really feeling the pressure of the All-Ireland. But all of this hullabaloo means we can just train and focus on the game!'

That made Jason feel better. But it was still hard for him to deal with all the attention. He'd spent his childhood being told how different he was. Now he was everyone's hero.

There were some good things that came with the attention.

The day before the game, Jason got a phone call.

'Jason, this is Martin Leung,' the voice said. It was his dad's brother. 'I just wanted to let you know we are all so proud of you! Granny Leung is a Gaelic football fan now!'

'Thank you Martin!' Jason said. They chatted for ten minutes. Jason's dad had moved out of the country, to South Africa. It was great to reconnect with his dad's side of the family. It was so nice of him to call.

Before leaving church, Jason remembered to pray for his beloved teammate Charlie Redmond. Mick and Jason were playing a game of pool Friday evening when they got word that Charlie had suffered a leg injury during training.

'He's 50-50 to play,' Mick said.

'Oh no, we can't lose Charlie,' Jason said.

'Who's going to take the frees if he can't play?' Mick said.

'It won't be me anyway!' Jason said with a laugh.

After mass, things happened very quickly. The bus to Croke Park. The warm up. The handshake with President Mary Robinson. The parade behind the Artane Band. Jason wore the number 14 jersey and was second last on the parade. Tyrone brought thousands of supporters down from the north, but the Dublin supporters owned Hill 16. As the parade approached the Hill, hundreds of blue flags began to wave. It was a sea of blue. It was one of the most beautiful things Jason had ever seen in his young life.

Within a blink of an eye, the ball had been thrown in and Jason was playing in the All-Ireland football final. It was a beautiful Sunday afternoon in September.

Tyrone had their own young star wearing the number 14 jersey. His name was Peter Canavan. Even though he was just twenty-four, the Tyrone supporters called him 'Peter the Great'.

The opening exchanges were cagey. Tyrone weren't going to lie down. Dublin were nervous.

It was a real ding-dong battle. Dublin lead 0-6 to 0-5 after twenty-five minutes. Jason was waiting for his moment to explode into the game. And then he spotted it. Bealo played a long ball up towards the full-forward line. Jason had been hanging a bit deeper, and sprinted towards the ball. The pass was intended for Mick Galvin, but the Tyrone defender cleaned it up – only to fumble the ball right into Jason's path! Jason sprinted on to the dirty ball and just nudged it forward with his foot.

The ball dropped into a no-man's land ten metres from goal. It was an all-out sprint for the ball between Jason and the Tyrone half back and the Tyrone keeper to get to the ball first. Jason was the farthest away, but he was also the fastest of the three.

'Dig deep,' he said to himself. He sprinted with every fibre of his being.

He knew it would be hard to score from here, but he knew any contact with the ball could lead to a goal. He dove and the Tyrone keeper dove at the same time. Jason's shot was blocked, but the ball fell right into the path of Charlie, who bundled it over into the net. Goal for the Dubs!

Jason didn't score the goal, but it couldn't have

been scored without him.

Dublin went into half time with a narrow lead.

'We just need to hold on lads!' Dr Pat said.

But Tyrone would not surrender. Charlie was sent off and Tyrone were relentless, but in the end, Dublin were crowned All-Ireland champions of 1995. They won the Sam Maguire for the first time in twelve years! Jason wasn't even twenty years old and he was already an All-Ireland winner.

After the match, there was a banquet at the Croke Park Hotel. Jason put on the team suit. *The Sunday Game* was filmed live from the hotel. Jason did an interview with Marty Morrissey.

It was unreal. Two years ago, Jason wasn't even a member of a Dublin GAA club. Now he was an All-Ireland winner at just nineteen. It was like a fairy tale.

Everyone was patting him on the back and telling him how brilliant he was. Every now and again, he'd hear a bunch of lads singing the 'Jayo' song.

It wasn't just that he was an All-Ireland winner. He was a phenomenon. Never in his wildest dreams could he have dreamed of this when he was back playing Wembley in Carrigallen Park.

In the hotel lobby, later that night, he met Kevin Moran.

'Kevin, the first time I met you was the last time Dublin won the All-Ireland twelve years ago! I was just a young lad in my communion suit!' Jason said.

'It's mad isn't it,' Kevin said. 'Savour it, because it's the best feeling in the world.'

'I know, it's amazing,' Jason said.

'Listen, Jason,' Kevin said. 'I've heard back from Liverpool. They'd be happy for you to come over for a trial. If you were up for it,' Kevin said.

'Oh my God,' Jason said. One of the biggest teams in English football was interested in him. It was a lot to process.

'You don't have to decide right now,' Kevin said. 'But at some stage, you're going to have to decide whether you want to chase that dream or stay here with the Dubs.'

'Okay, Kevin, thanks I'll think about it,' Jason said. It was one of the biggest decisions he'd have to make in his life. He listened to his head and his head told him that trying to break into a Premiership side was going to be very, very difficult. Even if the trial went well, he was not guaranteed he'd ever get a game with Liverpool.

He listened to his heart and his heart told him he was a true-blue Dub. After the amazing adventure that the Dublin team had been on this year, how could he turn his back on them?

When he woke up the next morning, the amazing feeling was still there.

'Well Jason, what will you do next?' his mam asked.

'My heart is in Dublin,' he said. 'And I want to continue being a Dublin Gaelic footballer.'

His mam gave him a big hug. She looked so proud.

EPILOGUE

The year was 2019. It was the day of the All-Ireland final replay. Jason Sherlock was heading to Croke Park.

The Dublin footballers were on the verge of a historic achievement in the GAA. If they beat Kerry in the All-Ireland replay, they'd complete a five-in-a-row.

No men's team in intercounty football or hurling had ever won the five-in-a-row before. Jason had had a front-row seat for the whole journey. He had been an assistant under head coach Jim Gavin for five years.

As he drove to meet the team and head to Croke Park, Jason thought back on his own sporting career as a player. He'd never again got up those sacred Hogan Stand steps to claim an All-Ireland medal, but he'd won seven Leinster titles. He'd captained his county. He'd soldiered with Dublin for fifteen seasons. He'd played in some amazing games. He'd made lifelong friends. He'd always be a cult hero to GAA supporters because of his heroics in 1995.

He still loved playing soccer. He'd had a few great years playing with Shamrock Rovers while playing for the Dubs.

Basketball kept a special place in his heart as well and he stayed in touch with Joey to see who the next great basketball player from St Vincent's would be.

Jason was a coach now: Dublin's forwards' coach, an assistant to his old teammate Jim Gavin. Coaching was a lot different to playing!

When Jason broke through with Dublin, he was a bit of a messer. Now he was a mentor for the lads. He'd always been a great student of the game. He loved taking learnings from sports like basketball and giving them to the Gaelic football team. And while Jason would have loved to have won as many All-Ireland medals as the Dublin players he coached now, he loved being a coach. Win today and it would be clear that Dublin were the best team of all time.

Eventually, the autograph hunters left him alone. The attention was nice during the crazy days of 1995, but fame wasn't all it was cracked up to be. He was recognised everywhere he went in Ireland, but after a while, Jason realised his nan was right. Education was the most important thing in life. Jason received a degree from DCU, and he now worked at the university in the area of education. He was so proud of DCU's Write To Read initiative, which helped boys and girls from disadvantaged areas continue their education at DCU.

Through it all, Jason developed a great appreciation for the things that mattered most in his life. Family. Sport. Dublin.

Jason had changed a lot over the years, and so had Ireland. As the team bus neared Croke Park, Jason looked out at the streets of Dublin, and there were people from all over the world walking and talking and shopping. It was a totally different country to the one he grew up in. It was normal now to come from Hong Kong or Poland or Nigeria and grow up in Finglas.

It had been hard growing up as the only kid who looked different in his school, but now he could help other young Irish kids. He was proud that the GAA was doing its part in helping Ireland to become more open and welcoming.

Unfortunately, racism hadn't gone away, but it was so important that the GAA had become a place where people from all backgrounds and nationalities belonged. Jason was living proof of that.

Minutes later he was out on the Croke Park pitch, watching the Dublin team go through their warm-up. The anticipation was growing on Hill 16. He knew they'd win today. On their day, Dublin were impossible to beat and Jason could tell from the intensity of the warm-up that this was their day.

For a brief second, Jason closed his eyes and imagined he was back in 1995, a young lad, fearless and a little bit bold, taking on the whole world. He had two kids of his own now and he knew they were in the stands, dreaming of playing for Dublin, just like he once did.

And in his head, he could hear the chant ring

out 'Boom, boom, boom, let me hear you say – Jayo!'

He smiled. What times he'd had.

JASON SHERLOCK'S
ACHIEVEMENTS

All-Ireland winner with Dublin, 1995

Seven-time Leinster football champion

Assistant coach for Dublin Gaelic football team, winning five All-Irelands.

Ireland under-21 soccer international

Represented Ireland internationally in basketball.

GREAT IRISH SPORTS STARS

ALSO AVAILABLE

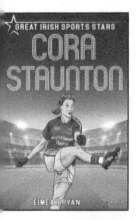

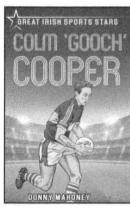

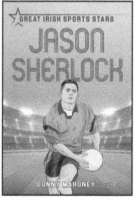